WITHDRAWN

WISDOM'S PRIZE

Other books by Patricia DeGroot:

A Will of Her Own
A Worth to Behold
A Place for Her Heart
Honor's Reward

WISDOM'S PRIZE

•

Patricia DeGroot

AVALON BOOKS
NEW YORK

Published by Thomas Bouregy & Co., Inc.
160 Madison Avenue, New York, NY 10016

Library of Congress Cataloging-in-Publication Data

DeGroot, Patricia.
    Wisdom's prize / Patricia DeGroot.
        p. cm. — (The Wilde flowers romance series)
    ISBN 0-8034-9746-6 (acid-free paper)
    1. Colorado—Fiction. I. Title. II. Series: DeGroot,
Patricia. Season of the Wilde flowers romance.

PS3554.E423W57 2005
813'.6—dc22

                                        2005007648

PRINTED IN THE UNITED STATES OF AMERICA
ON ACID-FREE PAPER
BY HADDON CRAFTSMEN, BLOOMSBURG, PENNSYLVANIA

To my one and only love.
Thirty-one years and counting.

And to seasons of change.

Chapter One

Autumn, Colorado 1875

Red had him this time.

Trip Dawson had claimed he wouldn't be in school today because he was helping his uncle work on their new barn. Instead, the boy was climbing the big ol' oak on the bank of the Platte River outside town.

On this cool and breezy November afternoon, on her way home from Ruley's schoolhouse, she'd been pondering the news she'd heard about widower Michael Wisdom when she'd come upon Trip high up in the leafless tree. Her disposition had already been irritable. First, there had been the gloomy news that Elias Burton, the school board superintendent had delivered to her this morning. The disturbing news about Mr.

1

Wisdom had compounded it. Now, seeing Trip, knowing he'd lied to her, made Red fit to be tied.

The scamp, she fumed.

Thoughts of Burton and Mr. Wisdom—the arrogant, if handsome—Mr. Wisdom, stalled, and she tugged on Honey's reins, scrambled out of her buggy, and strode down the river's embankment before Trip knew she was coming. At the base of the tree, her ankles deep in fall leaves, she placed her hands on her hips and stared upward.

"Working hard on that new barn are we, Mr. Dawson?" her voice carried through the dormant branches.

Startled, the boy's bare foot slipped. He quickly curled his toes around the trunk, grabbed hold of a thick branch, and looked down at her.

"So much for pounding nails, hmmm?" Red pursed her lips, almost wishing he'd fallen straight into the cold stream behind her.

Trip's eyes widened. "We . . . we got done earlier than I thought we would, Miss Meredith," the gangly boy stammered. He was taller than Red by a foot when he had his feet on the ground. A rare occurrence lately. Until this school term he'd been one of her better pupils. But now he couldn't seem to sit still in class, when he bothered to come to class, and two discussions with his uncle about his absenteeism had been met with disdain.

"Finished early?" she replied with a bit too much sarcasm lacing her schoolteacher's voice. "And you were headed straight for class, weren't you?"

"Well, er . . ."

Red sighed in frustration. She hated the fact that Trip was losing his desire to learn. He'd shown such potential over the last two years. And he wasn't the only student faltering lately. The Miller twins and even eight–year–old Nelly Erickson were struggling. Red was beginning to wonder if she was the reason the children were losing interest in their studies. Had the fact that she'd become disheartened with Superintendent Burton begun to rub off on her students?

She didn't want them to know about the problems she had with him and the two other committee members that oversaw the school. She'd done her best to hide her irritation. But since, in the past, she'd never received anything but thanks from Ruley's townsfolk for her efforts to educate their children, the current lack of funds and Burton's apathetic response to the situation rattled her.

"Come down from there," she called to Trip, and then counted silently to six before the boy complied. He landed at her feet with a thud and looked down at her with a dirt–smudged face and big brown eyes.

Red tilted her head back so she could see him. He was all of thirteen years but taller than most men. She wasn't about to let his height intimidate her. "You be in class tomorrow morning or I'll come find you," she ordered with an authority that defied her much smaller frame. "You arrive an hour early. For the next two weeks. You have several missed assignments to make up."

Trip's knobby shoulders drooped. "Yes, ma'am," he mumbled.

"It's for your own good," she added with a twinge of remorse for her harshness. "I'm doing this because I care about you. You understand that, don't you?"

"Well, ummm, yeah." His bony bare foot toyed with a dry fall leaf. "But, ummm, if you cared about someone else instead, that would be fine."

Red rolled her eyes heavenward, her weariness getting the best of her. Maybe she should take his advice. Give up on teaching altogether. Elias had made it clear the town didn't much care whether she had chalk, books, or even enough wood in the stove to keep the children warm now that fall had set it.

Still . . . "As much as I'm tempted to do just that, Mr. Dawson," she replied, "Don't get your hopes up. Be on time. No excuses."

The boy sighed. "Yes, ma'am."

She marched back up the embankment, leaving Trip, but taking her frustration. Why didn't Trip's uncle see the importance of him attending class? It was men like Calvin Dawson, and the newcomer, Michael Wisdom, who made things so difficult.

Michael Wisdom.

Had his wife and son really died in a tragic accident the way Wanda Etherton claimed this morning? Wanda had heard that very story from Mr. Dortch when Wanda had gone to the mercantile yesterday. If so, that would explain some of Mr. Wisdom's aloofness.

Red could still see him standing on his porch the day she'd ridden out to his ranch four months ago to introduce herself and invite his daughter, Caroline, to school.

Chillingly handsome, with his cold brown eyes and firm set jaw, his light brown hair falling over his forehead in waves, he'd made Red shiver in the July heat. A more stern–faced man she'd never met. Nor one who intimidated her with just a look. One that said she wasn't welcome.

Red had meant to step out of her buggy and join the father and daughter on their wide front porch until she'd seen that look, heard him say, "Too busy for visitors, ma'am. Just state your business and be on your way."

She'd stayed where she was all right, wondering for the first time just who Michael Wisdom was. He'd arrived only weeks after his brother, Peter, was crushed to death by his horse. Reanne Wisdom, Peter's wife, had taken the railroad east right after her husband's funeral, and Michael had moved into Peter's vacant ranch house and assumed the reins of Peter's thriving cattle operation. Grumbling had quickly spread after he fired all the local hands, hired new help from as far away as Colorado Springs; from then on, he had kept to himself.

He hadn't brought along a wife, just an adorable daughter that Red had seen with him at the mercantile. When she'd introduced herself as the town schoolteacher, the girl had clung to her father's pant leg, her blue eyes sad, her shoulder–length, wispy brown hair blowing about her face. Red had asked if she'd like to attend class.

"Caroline will learn all she needs to from me," her father had said in a firm tone before the girl could answer for herself.

Red still fumed when she thought about the rude way he'd treated her and the injustice Wisdom was doing his daughter. She seemed to think about it all too often. Especially after someone said something about him, like Wanda had today, or after seeing him in town lifting supplies into his wagon, his eyes downcast to dissuade anyone from talking to him. Caroline was always nearby. He never seemed to let her out of his sight.

Once, Red had stumbled into the child, who was admiring newly arrived dress fabrics. Caroline hadn't responded when Red asked her how she was, but she had coaxed a smile from her before her father had called her in an almost panic-stricken voice. Caroline's eyes had widened and she'd raced off to find him. Red had heard him scold her for disappearing.

She disliked the man immensely. More than Elias, who was just annoying. More than Trip's uncle, who was just plain ignorant. Michael Wisdom was much more complicated. So much so that she couldn't get her mind off him. Now that Wanda had told her about his wife and son, she wondered if his mean spirit had been born from such an awful loss. If so, she could almost understand why he didn't want Caroline out of his sight.

Wanda hadn't known anything more about the tragedy or how the accident had occurred, or where, or when. So she'd succeeded in only further stirring Red's mind with thoughts of the mystery man, fruitless thoughts that had kept her on edge since their first encounter.

She wished Wanda had never told her about Mr. Wisdom's tragedy. The last thing she needed was to feel sympathy for the man after his insolence. Even if he had lost his wife and son, it didn't give him the right to be so discourteous. Her seventeen students, ages six to fourteen, should be all she was thinking about. Why, tonight she had papers to grade, assignments to prepare, and what with Christmas just around the corner, she needed to concentrate on which students she was going to choose for rolls in the nativity pageant this year. Then, time permitting, she needed to figure out how she was going to find the money to pay for the rest of this term's supplies.

She could still hear Elias claiming he just didn't have any extra funds to spare, that he and the other members of the committee had voted down her request. Of course, he'd also made it clear that if she'd consent to have dinner with him next Saturday night, he might, just might, be able to sway them differently. She'd frowned at the bribe. Elias was considered a fine catch by most of the women in town. He was handsome, prominent, educated, and he seemed to achieve everything he attempted, but he was learning he wouldn't succeed in his goal to marry Red. She knew why he wanted to marry her, and it had nothing to do with love; he wasn't even attracted to her. No, Elias had made it clear that he wanted to marry her because it would align him with her well-respected family—a family that included the town doctor, blacksmith, and the largest horse ranch around. He was sure that alliance would assist him when he ran for mayor.

It amazed Red that he didn't understand why she didn't find his reason flattering.

She glanced over her shoulder one last time to see Trip climbing the tree again. She sank into the seat of her buggy. Darn Elias Burton, Trip's uncle, and Michael Wisdom anyway!

Maybe her life would be easier if she gave up her crusade to educate the children of Ruley and applied for a position at a university. It would be quite amusing if she were to become a teacher at Elias' former school. Of course, it could take months to land an interview with any university. She was a woman, after all. Which left her no choice but to deal with her current problems. She'd just go home and bury herself in piles of work that would keep her unproductive thoughts at bay.

The snap of several branches, a thud, and a grunt changed her plans. Her head swiveled back to the tree. At its base, Trip lay in a heap.

"Trip!" she called. She raced back down the embankment, stumbling and sliding until she reached his side. "Are you all right?" she asked, falling to her knees.

The boy moaned, his face tight with pain. When he tried to move, Red added, "Stay still. We don't want to make anything worse."

"M-my arm," he mouthed, and writhed. "I think it's broke." As he grabbed the limb with his other hand, Red saw the protruding bone.

"Dear Lord," she whispered. She added, "All right, don't move," and then glanced around, but saw nothing but riverbank, dormant trees, and autumn grass. "I'll be right back." She climbed the bank once more, wishing she hadn't chosen today of all days to wear her new boots. They had a higher heel than her other boots, and the narrower toe on the steep climb was beginning to pinch her feet.

When she reached her buggy, she peered inside. She decided her cloak could cushion Trip's arm, and the drawstring from her reticule, if she wrapped it around the cloak, would keep it in place.

She emptied her bag on the seat and then took a moment to glance up and down the road, hoping someone was nearby that could assist them. Unfortunately, there was no one, so she hurried back to Trip. She heard his moaning before she reached him. "I'm coming," she encouraged. "Try to stay calm. We'll get you into town and I'm sure Doc Travis will have you patched up in no time. Try to hold still while I wrap my cloak around you."

She gently wound the wool garment around Trip's arm and the purse's long drawstrings around the cloak, and then waited a moment to see if the pain would subside. "There. How does that feel?" she said as the empty bag perched on top of the cloak. "Is that any better?" The boy blinked several times before his eyes seemed to focus. His breathing eased as well.

"I can't believe I fell like that," he said, clearly surprised by his own limitations.

Red frowned. Were all males so arrogant? But she was relieved his pain had subsided. "Can you stand up? Come on. Let's get you into town."

She struggled to help him to his feet, waited until she was sure his pain was still under control, and then steered him up the embankment towards the road. They were halfway up the rise, and she was sweating from the effort, when movement caught her eye. She glanced up to see a man standing at the edge of the bank looking down at them.

Mr. Wisdom, of all people.

She couldn't help but consider the moment surreal. How was it that the irritable man of her irritable thoughts had arrived at that particular place at that particular time? Worse, vanity was rearing its ugly head, making her wonder just what she must look like now that she'd traipsed up and down the Platte's bank. She shoved the thought away, irritated with herself, even as she admitted that when it came to this man, her mind was always playing games with her.

"Have an accident?" he asked in the cool, collected voice she detested.

Disgusted with herself, she shoved her vanity aside and instead calculated the consequences of not answering him. It would have been a fitting payback. He'd been boorish to her. Why couldn't she give him some of his own medicine?

Unfortunately, she needed his help. "Mr. Dawson fell out of a tree," she said. She made sure her own voice was calm and collected. "He broke his arm."

The man drew the back of his hand across his jaw as if assessing her news. But his hat lay low on his brow, shading his brown eyes and making it difficult to gage his reaction.

"I'm taking him to Dr. Worth," she added briskly when he said nothing more. She was practically pushing Trip up the steepest part of the incline, her breathing labored and her disposition worsening by the moment. She was just about to tell Mr. Wisdom to move his sorry self out of the way if he was just going to stand there, when he reached for Trip.

"Step aside," he said, as if she were the one in the way.

Red warred with her need to tell him what he could do with his order. But as winded as she was, and with Trip groaning again, she turned the boy over to him. "If you would just help him to my buggy," she said in between breaths, "I can manage from there."

"He'll be better off laying down in my wagon," Wisdom replied.

Patricia DeGroot

She stood on the bank, taking deep breaths. "Yes. Yes, he would." She couldn't believe he was offering the vehicle to them but, to her surprise, he led Trip to the back end.

Caroline was seated on the front bench, her finger in her mouth, her eyes wide. Red found a smile for her as she followed the girl's father.

"You're coming with me, aren't you, Miss Meredith?" Trip called over his shoulder, fear and pain mingling in his voice.

His words reminded Red of just how young and vulnerable he was. Her irritation diminished. "Of course, Trip. If you want me to."

"Yes ma'am," the boy grimaced.

His words further soothed her. Trip might not want her to teach him, but he apparently still held her in some regard. She slid by Mr. Wisdom with a curt, "Pardon me," and gathered the hem of her dark green skirt. She placed her aching foot on the wagon's hitch and unceremoniously hoisted herself into the wagon. She turned to assist Trip then, taking the boy's arm carefully into her hands as he climbed aboard. With a moan he sat down and she cautiously balanced his arm on his leg.

Once he was settled, she felt a hand on her own arm. Without needing to look, she knew Mr. Wisdom was holding her steady. Her breathing stilled. She fought away an urge to glance his way and instead used the leverage he offered to lower herself to the floorboard.

Once she was seated, she waited for him to release her. When he failed to do so, she did look at him. She saw he was looking at her as well. He quickly removed his hand, pivoted, and walked away. Shaky, Red touched the skin his hand had held. The area was warm, flushed. And spreading.

"Give me a minute to park your rig off the roadway," he said, startling her anew. "I'll unhitch your mare and tie her to my wagon."

Forcing air into her lungs, she scolded herself for reacting to his touch but told herself it was obviously due to the excitement of the afternoon. She would have never responded in kind under normal circumstances. She didn't like the man. His conduct—one moment as boorish as any man could be and the next as helpful— was just confusing her. It certainly wasn't because she was attracted to him. That was just plain unacceptable.

She watched as he tied Honey to the back of the wagon and grudgingly said, "Thank you. This is all very kind of you."

His only answer was to tip—just barely—the brim of his hat.

Red inwardly fumed. And yet she was relieved to have her tarnished image of him restored. She couldn't help but wonder if he'd always had such a dual person- ality or if the tragedy Wanda had referred to had changed him. Regardless, Mr. Wisdom was none of her business and he was going to stay that way. Within the hour they'd part company and return to their estranged acquaintance. She would be more than grateful when that moment occurred. Until then, she needed to focus her attention on Trip and not Michael Wisdom. "How are you feeling?" she asked the boy as he leaned his head against the wagon's sideboard. "Do you hurt anywhere else?"

Trip's voice squeaked as he said, "I'm okay, sorta. I climb that tree all the time. Can't believe I fell like that."

Red realized his ego was hurting more than anything. Still, she couldn't prevent one burnished brow from lifting, the teacher in her emerging in full form. "Well it just proves you should have been in school," she scolded. "If you'd been in class like you were supposed to, none of this would have happened."

Trip grimaced as the horses' movement shimmied the wagon. "Uncle Calvin says schoolin's for babes," he replied.

"He *what*?" Red saw red. "Why that good–for–nothing, illiterate . . . pig farmer. Is that why you haven't been attending class? Because your uncle ridicules learning? Oh, Trip," she sighed. "School is not for babes. School is for people who realize knowledge will take them where they could never go otherwise. How would we have railroads, electricity and new machines of every kind without discovery and ingenuity?" Her oft–stated words flowed effortlessly from her lips and purposely loud enough for Mr. Wisdom's ears. "Only fools despise wisdom and instruction," she lectured, gaining momentum. "It is the most basic of necessities. Education is what opens the door to hundreds of possibilities."

Michael fought to ignore the schoolmarm's homily as he climbed onto the wagon's front seat. Giving Caroline a half-smile, he patted her knee and took up his horses' reins. He set the pair moving toward town as he silently grumbled for stopping to help out in the first place. If he'd been a smarter man, he'd have ignored Miss Meredith Wilde's buggy parked on the road. He'd have driven right past it, told himself that nothing foul was taking place, that why it was there and where she might be was none of his concern.

The problem was that in another life the empty buggy would have signaled potential trouble, and as much as Claire and Daniel's deaths had changed him, some things remained the same. The hardness around his heart hadn't choked out all his common decency. He had a duty to make sure the lively, if over–rambunctious, teacher was all right.

Now though, he was paying the price.

It was apparent she was going to lecture the kid all the way to town and Michael would hear it all. It was nothing less than what he should have expected. She'd tried to do the same to him on the one occasion she'd called out at the ranch. His deliberate discourtesy had put a quick end to that, but he'd had a feeling she'd find a way to repay him.

He tried to mollify himself by reasoning she was just

passionate about her job. That was a good thing for the people of Ruley. He even admired it, despite everything. What he didn't admire was someone else's passion interfering in his life, like hers had the day she'd arrived at the ranch and invited Caroline to attend class. It had taken him days to get Caroline to stop pleading with him to change his mind. Miss Wilde hadn't appreciated his answer any more than Caroline had, and by the way her voice was carrying—deliberately, he was sure—she still didn't appreciate it.

He pitied himself and the boy, and almost turned around to advise Trip to save himself a lot of trouble and just play by her rules. But another, more shaded side of Michael wanted the boy to disagree. Even if the pretty Miss Wilde was right.

It was that shaded side that had taken root after the fire. Daniel had gone first, almost immediately after Michael had pulled him from the barn. His burns hadn't killed him. Doc said it was the bad air he'd breathed. Claire had lingered, though. For six torturous days. Her skin charred coal black from fighting the flames in an attempt to save their son.

Michael had determined that if she lived, he'd be able to rationalize Daniel's loss. She'd apologized repeatedly for not being able to save him. But as she'd breathed her last, while he held her in his arms, his anger had churned. Bitterness scorched him on the inside as surely as Claire's skin had been scorched on the outside.

Three years later, fire raged within him still, had left a permanent black scar around his soul. He hadn't forgiven himself for not being able to rescue his family. And he hadn't forgiven God either.

Today his vigilance would make certain that nothing of the like happened to his daughter, his only remaining reason for living. And no interfering small town schoolmarm with designs to save the world would tell him how to raise her.

On the few occasions his path had crossed with Miss Wilde in town—at the mercantile, in the bank, standing on the boardwalk—she'd been talking with folks about her school and its students.

It wasn't as if he'd been looking for her. But with that no–nonsense stride of hers, and with that incredible red-as-the-summer-sun-setting-over-the-Rocky-Mountains-and-just-as-untamable hair of hers, she was hard to miss.

She also had an infectious laugh, not that he heard it often or went out of his way to notice. It was just that the sound drew his attention. He'd decided it went along with her passionate nature.

She laughed now and Michael felt little pinpricks race along his skin. He glanced behind him, saw Trip Dawson squeeze Miss Wilde's hand, and knew her lecture hadn't fallen on deaf ears.

He had to look away. He concentrated on steering his team of horses around the ruts in the road.

"Is he going to be all right, Papa?" Caroline whispered from beside him.

Michael smiled again, his daughter's voice always a calming effect on his mood. "He'll be fine, Buttercup," he whispered back. "Boys like Trip always hurt themselves."

"Cause they're big bugs?"

Michael glanced at his daughter. "Where'd you hear that?"

"Deidre used to say so. About Daniel. She'd say he was a big bug."

Michael felt a pang in his chest even as he stifled a rare chuckle. "I think you mean big lug, Buttercup. 'Cause Daniel was clumsy. He used to stumble over himself all the time."

"The boy was a big lug, too, and fell out of the tree?" She continued to speak in a small voice, her pudgy, trusting hand on his thigh.

Michael patted her hand with a bittersweet sigh. If only Caroline could stay his little girl forever. "Yes, Buttercup. That's what he did." *Just like Daniel had done time and again.* Why hadn't his last act of defiance been nothing more than another close call? Why'd it have to steal Daniel's life?

"Do you know where Dr. Worth's office is, Mr. Wisdom?"

Michael was drawn back to the moment by Miss Wilde's question. "Caroline had a cold last month," he replied. He didn't bother turning his head to address her. "We've been there."

He could sense her tense with disapproval over the way he'd replied, and for some reason his surliness didn't settle well with him either. "It's just ahead," he added in a more moderate tone.

He steered the horses to the three–story building where Worth had his practice. Setting aside the reins, he turned to Caroline. "You wait for me right here," he said in the stern tone he'd come to use with her when he wanted her to know he was serious. "You don't leave this wagon until I come get you. Understand?"

"Yes, Papa." Caroline frowned and lowered her eyes.

Feeling that awful pang of guilt that was always with him when it came to his daughter, Michael lifted her chin. "I'll be right back, Buttercup," he said to soothe her.

Caroline smiled. Michael needed her smiles. They were about all that kept him going some days. He worried he was breaking her spirit by holding her so tightly, but it was either that or risk losing her. And he could never survive that.

He jumped down from the wagon seat and headed around back to watch Miss Wilde already rising to her feet. As she stood he couldn't help but notice the white ruffle of petticoat dancing around her ankles beneath her skirts.

"I'll go tell Travis we're here," she said. Before he

could assist her, she swung one foot over the tailgate, perched her boot on the narrow rail, and held onto the gate and tried to do the same with her other foot. She'd have been fine if her boot hadn't caught the top of the gate. Thrown off balance, she gasped as she began to fall. Michael scooped her up as she tumbled toward the ground.

"Oh!" she cried as she landed in his arms.

He grunted as her elbow grazed his chin. Her hair, so properly pinned beneath her dainty green hat, toppled from its confinement and spilled across his face.

A moment slid by silently. And then she moved her head, her hair sliding away from his face. He stared into a pair of shocked emerald eyes. The most brilliant pair of green eyes he'd ever seen.

Another moment slid by. She fit well in the cradle of his arms. She was lighter than he'd imagined, her hips and waist smaller than her skirts suggested. He had a close view of the small dimple in her cheek, of her ruby red lips, and of the blush creeping over her long neck and faint, freckle-dotted cheekbones.

He felt a sudden and inexplicable pull in the center of his gut just before guilt slammed into him.

"I–I–I'm so sorry," she stammered.

He tried to feign calmness as he set Miss Wilde on her feet and backed up a pace. Inside, he was furious with himself for betraying Claire so. "Go get the doctor," he ordered, his voice edgy.

She eyed him a moment, her irises intense, before hurrying away without a reply.

After she'd entered the building and disappeared, he took a deep breath, and then another, and finally felt his tension subside. There was no denying that Meredith Wilde was an enticing woman for a willing man.

He just wasn't willing.

He turned to Trip. "Come on, boy," he grumbled.

Trip just stared at him. "I–I can wait for Doc. You don't need to help no more."

The boy's frightened tone tugged at Michael's core. He cleared his throat and tried for civility. "Didn't mean to sound so churlish. I've no cause to be annoyed with you." Just a too–pretty schoolteacher. "Now come on. Let's get you inside."

Trip hesitated briefly before he scooted toward the tail.

"This your first break?" Michael asked him to further calm his anxiety, "I broke my arm when I was about your age."

The boy grinned from ear–to–ear, his fear dissolving. "Split my head wide open last summer when a bull threw me. Thought I broke my neck the time I jumped out of the hayloft, but it mended. This truly is my first break."

"Something tells me it won't be the last," Michael chuckled. He helped the boy steady himself.

"Fell out of a tree, Trip?"

Michael and the boy pivoted to see Travis Worth heading their way. Michael trusted the over–sized doctor, a competent, friendly man who didn't ask too many questions.

Miss Wilde, Michael saw, stayed near the building, her brows knit, her hands twined tightly together in front of her. She was intently watching Trip and Dr. Worth, but he could tell she still hadn't recovered from her tumble. He'd wager it wasn't every day something like this occurred in her life. Something had finally succeeded in silencing her! She'd fallen right off her high horse, straight . . . into his arms.

Michael swallowed tightly.

"Let's get you inside and have a look at you," Worth was saying to Trip. The doctor gingerly led the boy to his office. Miss Wilde held the door for them.

"You coming in Miss Meredith?" the boy asked.

"You'll be fine now, Trip." She patted his shoulder. "I need to get home before dark. Doc Travis will see you home after he sets your arm."

"Okay, then. Thanks for not leaving me."

Her gaze softened. "I'd never leave you, Trip."

"And Miss Meredith?"

"Yes, Trip?"

"I'll be in school tomorrow. Early."

Her face lit up with his words, a smile that had Michael sucking in his breath. Michael could feel her passion, her genuineness. She was a light in a dark world. There was no doubt about it.

"I'll be waiting for you, Trip," she replied. "See you tomorrow."

Her smile lingered after the doctor and boy had disappeared inside. Then she seemed to remember Michael. She glanced his way. He didn't pretend he hadn't been watching her as her smile slowly faded.

"I . . . I'll just get my horse," she said and headed toward Honey.

Michael reacted quickly and reached the horse before she did. He began to fiddle with the rope's knot that had the horse secured to the wagon.

"Thank you for all your help, Mr. Wisdom," he heard Miss Wilde say from beside him. "We . . . Mr. Dawson and I are very appreciative."

Michael continued working the knot.

"And thank you for . . . for catching my fall," she added hesitantly. She lifted a foot. "New boots."

"You plan to walk back to your rig in them?" he asked. Caroline gave him a strange look, along with Miss Wilde.

"I . . . I think I'll see if Luke can drive me back," she replied. She slid her slender hand along the mare's flanks. "If he hasn't left the smithy for the evening."

"Luke Hart? The blacksmith?" Michael felt his neck grow warm. He was still firing off questions he hadn't planned on asking. What was wrong with him? It had to be because he'd met the blacksmith. Another man he'd come to like, but a man Michael knew to be married.

Her hand paused on the mare's coat and he thought he

saw the briefest hint of a grin on her face. "Luke is married to my cousin, June," she answered. "Dr. Worth is married to her sister, May. Our fathers were brothers."

Well, that explained it. Feeling like a fool, Michael focused on the knot he was having so much difficulty loosening. It was his own fault he didn't know the connection between Miss Wilde and the others. He'd kept to himself since moving to the area and he planned to keep it that way. That's why his curiosity rankled. And yet her answer was satisfying.

"No need bothering your cousin," he said, discontinuing his efforts to untie the knot. "I have to pass by your rig on my way home anyway," he explained with what he hoped amounted to believable indifference. "No reason why you can't hitch a ride. I've got business at the bank first, but nothing that will keep me long."

Her pretty oval face continued to show her surprise, but it couldn't have been more than Michael's own.

"I . . . ah . . . all right. I suppose . . ."

"Then again, if you'd rather pester your cousin—"

"No. I mean, that is . . . if there's no reason to bother him . . ."

He strode to the head of the wagon before she could change her mind. "I'll help you up beside Caroline then," he said and waited.

The smile she gave him was tentative. Just enough to reveal her dimple. Just enough to make his stomach knot again and his conscience spike.

"Just being neighborly," he said beneath his breath. He wasn't sure if he was trying to convince her or himself.

She said nothing when he cupped her elbow, but he felt her shaking. From fear, disdain, or something else entirely he didn't know, but he'd asked enough questions. He couldn't believe what he'd gotten himself into. Especially since he had no one to blame but himself.

She settled next to Caroline and heard her draw a deep breath. "It's good to see you again, Caroline," she said then. "How are you?"

"I have a new doll baby," Caroline told her. "She has red hair like you."

Michael climbed into the driver's seat, deciding to accede the conversation to the females. He'd spouted off enough for one day. Since losing his wife and son, he'd deliberately kept his distance from people. Getting too close stung. He didn't plan on getting stung ever again.

He hadn't had a problem keeping his unwritten rule until today. So what made today different? Why had he offered the stuffy schoolmarm a ride? Why her, of all people?

Chapter Two

"And what did you name your new doll?" Red asked Caroline, struggling to concentrate on her conversation with the child; her mind was too occupied with thoughts of the girl's father instead. She could still see herself falling into his arms. She could remember being held in those arms, strong arms that had embraced her tightly, stopped her fall. She'd looked into his dark eyes, seen that they were shadowed and yet strangely clear. And she'd felt the warmth of him, his frame solid and firm. Even now his warmth lingered just as his hands had lingered on her skin. Had she imagined that he'd held her for just a moment longer than was necessary?

Still reeling from the event, and from his offer to take her back to her buggy, it was difficult to pay full

26

attention to his daughter. But Red fought down an urge to look over Caroline's head at him and focused on Caroline. The child didn't deserve to be slighted. "When I was your age I had a doll too. Her name was Annie and she was my best friend," she added.

Caroline stared up at her, her face cherubic. She had the faint look of her father, except that her eyes were the bluest of blues, and her hair, so shiny and flyaway, was the soft color of wheat. "I haven't named my doll yet. I've been trying. Maybe you could help me."

Red squeezed her small hand. "I'd love to help you pick a name for your doll," she replied. She'd welcome any distraction that would help take her mind off Michael Wisdom and the events of the last hour. Unfortunately, she didn't think anything could. "What names have you considered?"

"Well, I thought of all the names that begin with A," Caroline confessed. "Like Annie. But I didn't like any of them."

"You know your letters?" Red blinked, jolted by the statement. How did Caroline know her alphabet if her father didn't allow her to attend school? No longer fighting her urge to glance his way, she did so, and saw him grin rather broadly.

"'Course I know my letters," Caroline replied matter–of–factly. "I'm eight. Papa taught them to me when I was six."

"Six. Yes." Red felt heat creep into her cheeks. She'd assumed the girl was unschooled. An assumption, she realized now, she had no right to make. And her father had taught her. "All right then," she said. "Shall we think of some names that begin with B?"

"There's Belinda and Betty," Caroline said. "And Buttercup, but that's my special name, isn't it, Papa?"

He smiled and Caroline tugged on his sleeve, signaling for him to lower his head. When he'd complied, she whispered, "Miss Wilde is pretty, Papa, isn't she?"

His smile faded. "She is, Buttercup," he whispered back. "But your mama was the prettiest woman in the world."

Oh Lord! Red thought to herself, mortified. "Belinda is nice," she managed, pretending she hadn't heard the exchange. Even so, she wanted to jump from the wagon. An ache formed in the center of her chest. Suddenly feeling like an intruder, she wondered what had possessed her to join them in the first place. She hadn't wanted to seem impolite. He'd claimed she'd be pestering Luke. But seated there on the bench seat, with him telling his daughter how pretty her mother had been, she had to admit she'd *wanted* to prolong her departure. For just a little while.

How foolish she'd been. The man must have loved his wife very much. If Caroline's features were any indication, her mother had had a classic look. Had Red thought there was even a remote possibility that Mr. Wisdom might find her, with her freckled-face and carrot-hued hair, attractive?

Fool, she chided herself. She was in sadder shape

than she'd realized. Mr. Wisdom was hard, cold. Brutal. Why, she'd disliked him from the onset. He was worse than Elias Burton! And yet, she'd wanted to be in his company.

"There's also Beatrice or Bernice." Red inhaled long and slowly. *You know, Lord, I could really use some help here.*

She decided to leave once they arrived at the bank. She'd claim she just remembered she had an errand to run. Once she was away, she'd head to the livery and have Luke take her to her buggy as previously planned. And if Luke was too busy, if she had to walk all the way alone, she would do so. Anything was preferable to staying put.

"How about Beth?" Caroline said without an inkling to Red's turmoil. Red gave the girl a smile. Any other time she would have enjoyed Caroline's company and been able to give the child her undivided attention. She was bright and friendly and obviously in need of some female companionship.

As it was now, Red was focused on escape.

Thankfully, Mr. Wisdom was pulling the rig up to the bank. She stayed on the bench seat as he reined the horses and jumped to the ground. She was going to wait until he and Caroline were entering the bank before calling out that she had a forgotten errand of her own to run. She'd be gone before he could reply. If he thought to reply at all. With him, she didn't know what to expect.

"We'll be back in a few minutes," he said and began to lift Caroline down with him.

She backed away from his reach. "I want to stay with Miss Wilde," the girl protested.

Mr. Wisdom eyed his daughter with a lifted brow, clearly surprised by her action.

"Please, Papa. You'll only be gone a few minutes and we were naming my baby doll." She pivoted toward Red. "Will you show me how to braid my hair? I want to braid Beth's hair, but I don't know how."

"But—" Red gazed down at the child, tenderness washing over her. How could she leave when Caroline wanted her to stay? How could she leave when the child merely wanted—needed—a few minutes with her?

She reluctantly shifted her gaze to Caroline's father. She instantly wished she hadn't. His eyes revealed the hurt of Caroline's rejection. That, coupled with his rugged handsomeness, was too much for her senses.

He was dangerous. In ways she'd never experienced before and didn't know how to fight. It was no wonder she couldn't stop thinking about him. Clearly her concern for Caroline had been overlaid with concern for him too. She had felt there was sorrow in his life long before Wanda's revelation about his wife and son.

She averted her gaze from his shadowed eyes—old eyes—and waited for his response to his daughter's request.

"You have long hair, don't you?" Caroline's chipper voice broke through the tension. It was warily confident, like she wasn't quite sure her father would give in to her request. "I can tell cause you have so much piled under your hat. I want real long hair one day. Papa cuts mine now so it won't tangle. But when I'm old like you, I'm gonna let it grow and I'll brush it and brush it so it shines like yours."

Red's heart melted further. She cupped Caroline's chin and couldn't stop herself from looking at Mr. Wisdom again, from imploring him on her behalf. "I'll watch her very closely," she said. "She won't leave the seat."

His mouth thinned, his eyes hardened, but he stared back at her, and she knew that he knew she understood his fear. "You'll listen to Miss Wilde?" he asked Caroline.

"Yes, Papa." Caroline tensed, waiting, even as she began to play with strands of her own hair.

"I won't be long, but—"

"I promise, Papa. I won't go anywhere. Miss Wilde won't let me. I'll be right here when you come back." The eight–year–old seemed older by years for a moment.

"She's safe with me, Mr. Wisdom," Red further assured him, but she could still see the battle he was waging. A battle for control. Or maybe one to relinquish control.

His gaze pierced hers again. His straight nose flared. If something did happen to his daughter while he was away, his wrath would know no bounds. Red knew she was taking a risk by trying to make Caroline happy.

Even so, she watched him nod, turn. His stride was

purposeful but not hurried despite his inner–battle. And she was mesmerized by the width of his shoulders beneath his white shirt and brown overcoat, mesmerized by the ends of his sun–lightened hair curling at the edge of his collar as she waited for him to glance back to check on his daughter. Instead, he disappeared into the bank's interior without even a glance.

"Miss Wilde?"

Red blinked, then smiled down at the child. "Yes, Caroline, my hair is long. Sometimes it tangles too. Shall we braid your hair now? I'll show you how it's done."

His deposit made, Michael paused to peer out the bank windows as he made his way toward the exit and caught sight of Caroline and Miss Wilde right where he'd left them not ten minutes earlier.

Taking a deep breath, he exhaled his anxiety and continued through the door. The temperature had begun to dip and the day's shadows were lengthening, but he barely noticed. His attention remained on the two females seated in his wagon. He was still a bit miffed with his daughter for wanting to stay with Miss Wilde. Granted, having a woman to talk to was new and different, but she'd always looked forward to their visits to the bank before and the licorice stick the teller always had for her.

The teller had given Michael the candy anyway. Michael had it in his coat pocket. He'd give it to his daughter later—when she snuggled up to him. She always snuggled up to him after pleading to go somewhere or do something he didn't much care for. She'd come to him afterward, tell him she wasn't mad at him anymore and then give him a big hug. That's when he'd give her something special—like her new doll. Or the candy.

She was bright, his buttercup. She understood why she couldn't do some of the things the other children did.

Like attend school.

She also knew he'd given in to her plea to stay with Miss Wilde because the risk was minimal. Had danger threatened, he'd have been able to reach her quickly. Something he hadn't been able to do when his wife and son needed him. He'd promised himself he'd never be too far away again, even if that meant his daughter would suffer occasionally for it.

This time he'd been able to accommodate her. His displeasure had been short–lived and continued to all but evaporate when he saw the easy smile on her face. The schoolteacher was fiddling with her hair. Miss Wilde said something that made Caroline laugh. The sound was sweet and lyrical. A good sound that made his walk lighter. Miss Wilde laughed with Caroline and it swirled around him.

Seeing his daughter made him glad he'd offered the teacher a ride. He still couldn't say what had prompted him. He didn't want to know and wasn't going to try and figure it out. But at least his knee-jerk invitation had proved beneficial for Caroline.

He couldn't say the same for himself.

Red saw him emerge from the bank. She barely had time to redirect her gaze back to Caroline's hair before he caught her looking at him.

Her cheeks heating, she admitted she'd been on pins and needles ever since he'd disappeared inside. All the time she'd been visiting with Caroline and twisting her hair into a braid, thoughts of Caroline's father remained front and center.

Not that Red wanted to think about him. The man was like a burr in a dog's paw; a sore spot. One that gnawed. And she couldn't wait to remove the burr. Unfortunately, that meant he had to return if she was ever to get back to her buggy.

"Papa!" Caroline exclaimed when she, too, noticed his approach. "You weren't gone very long, Papa. Look at my hair. Do you like it?"

The wagon swayed as he climbed aboard. He sat down and eyed Caroline's new style. Then he took Caroline's chin in hand and turned her face one way, then another.

Caroline giggled and Red couldn't help but smile. Then he smiled too, and Red's insides did a somersault.

"You're prettier than ever, Buttercup," he told her and kissed her nose.

Caroline continued to giggle. He glanced at Red. For

a moment they smiled at each other. Then abruptly his smile dimmed and he turned his attention to the horses. "What did you talk about while I was gone?" he asked.

Caroline looked to her with a conspiratorial grin before she leaned into her father. "Girl things," she whispered.

"Girl things, huh?" he pressed.

"Caroline and I were just talking about our favorite colors," Red told him. She smoothed a few loose strands of Caroline's hair into the braid and tried to breath. "Caroline said she liked the color pink so we agreed we needed a bit of pink lace to help her braid stay in place." She released the twined ends to prove her point and watched the locks quickly unravel.

"Oh no," Caroline cried on another laugh.

"We'll have to braid your hair again when we have that ribbon," Red soothed.

Caroline fingered her straight tresses. "Today? Can we go to Mr. Dortch's? Don't you have more business you can do, Papa?"

"Sorry, Buttercup, not this time."

"But—"

"There will be another time," Red tried to appease her.

"Tomorrow then?" Caroline pestered.

Red wasn't about to make that commitment even though Caroline needed a woman in her life. Her father had to realize that. It would do a world of good for them both if he found someone to fill the void.

Someone.

But not her. Definitely not her.

"I'm sure Miss Wilde is busy tomorrow," he answered.

"But, Papa—"

"Hold on now." He interrupted. "We need to get moving." His accommodating tone had disappeared. The horses lurched forward as Caroline's shoulders slumped.

Red placed an arm around the child and smiled reassuringly when she peered up at her with sad eyes. Having seen the gentleness he used when dealing with her, Red convinced herself he'd soon shift his stance again and give in to Caroline's request. But a short time later they were pulling alongside Red's buggy right where she'd abandoned it and Mr. Wisdom was jumping down from the seat, making a dash to untie her horse, Honey. Without a word, he began to harness her to the buggy.

Red's irritation with him resurfaced. The man had more sides to him than an octagon, a surly side being one of them. Climbing down from the wagon, she faced Caroline and said, "I enjoyed visiting with you today." She gently squeezed her arm. "I'm sure your father will let us visit again soon. Then we'll finish braiding your hair."

"Tomorrow?" the girl pleaded again.

"You're all set." Mr. Wisdom's voice carried across the road. He was holding Honey's reins, his impatience noticeable.

Red frowned anew. His rudeness was in full bloom again. He was acting as if *she'd* asked *him* for a ride. And was he so blind? Was he going to continue to ignore his daughter's needs? Caroline wanted a woman's company. She wasn't asking for anything outlandish.

As much as Red wanted her ordeal with Mr. Wisdom to end, as much as she knew she was going to regret her next words, she said to the girl, "How about Saturday?" Then she marched over to the man, yanked Honey's reins from his hand and ground out, "Thank you. I'm sorry you've been so inconvenienced today. In the future, if you see me on the roadside, please be assured it's not necessary to stop.

"However, I'm sure you realize the afternoon was not a complete loss. Caroline, if no one else, enjoyed herself. And since I'm a firm believer in fate, I'm wondering if Trip's tumble from the tree was to show you that your daughter is in dire need of some female companionship."

When her words failed to stir a response, Red pursed her lips and went on. "My cousin April has a daughter just a couple of years younger than Caroline. Sarah could benefit from a friendship with Caroline as much as Caroline could. It just so happens that I'm tending Sarah on Saturday. I'll arrive at your home around one with Sarah so the girls can play together."

She turned away from him then, neither waiting for an answer or a reaction. She certainly wasn't going to wait to see if he would do the gentlemanly thing and help her into her buggy. It was apparent he turned on and off his manners at whim, and she wasn't about to set herself up for another disappointment.

"Good-bye, Caroline," she said when she was seated. Her voice was calm while her insides rattled. "I'll see you in a few days and I'll bring you a new friend. We'll have a nice visit then." She glanced at Mr. Wisdom with a challenge in her eye, daring him to protest. Again, he said nothing.

"Good day, sir," she said. Honey took off then and Red never looked back. The sun was rapidly descending and she still had papers to grade, lessons to develop and a hundred other chores to do when she got home. It was time she focused on those things, rather than the infuriating man she'd just left behind.

Chapter Three

Three days later, Red dismissed class with relief, glad the school day was over. Exhaustion had set in yesterday after two sleepless nights. At this point, she was surprised she could still stay on her feet.

She had only herself to blame for her predicament. She still couldn't believe she had actually told Michael Wisdom that on Saturday she was going to bring Sarah to his house to play with Caroline.

Saturday. Tomorrow.

What in the world had she been thinking?

She'd had no plans to tend Sarah. Her plans had been to attend the Ruley Women's Charity Alliance luncheon.

Furthermore, why hadn't he refused? He'd never had a difficult time stating his mind before.

She stacked papers on her desk into a pile and scooted her chair back while she continued to admonish herself. This wasn't the first time her bravado had gotten her into trouble. The year she'd turned ten she'd punched a boy for throwing rocks at a neighborhood cat. He'd punched her back, leaving her with a black eye. Then there had been the time, years later, when she'd watched old Mrs. Spencer's reticule get snatched. Red had shouted an alarm and raced after the culprit— only to have him trip her, sending her sprawling on the boardwalk. Her own purse had skittered out of her reach. She could still see the devious smile on the boy's face when he had scooped it up and ran off.

More recently, she had held her ground with Elias Burton and had to wonder what the consequences were going to be because of that. Her sister, Kit, claimed Red's temper complimented her hair color. And that she hadn't earned her nickname for nothing. Most of the time she was proud of that fact. Today it was cause for self–examination.

What else could she have done, though, but give Caroline what her father wouldn't? And what else could she do now but keep her word? She'd told Caroline she'd see her on Saturday. She'd said she'd bring a playmate. Red had already known she wouldn't renege on her promise, so last night, after school, she'd gone to ask her cousin, April, if April's daughter, Sarah, could spend tomorrow afternoon with her. April was the oldest of her three cousins. She and her husband

Will lived on a horse ranch not far from Ruley. May and June were April's sisters. They had all lived in the cabin Red lived in now before they each married. Now they all had children as well. April's oldest was Sarah and named after her mother. The soon-to-be six-year-old had beamed at the prospect of making a new friend. Sarah was a friendly girl and had cousins and a sibling to play with, but they were all boys.

Red agreed to have her back by three–thirty. And April hadn't pried into how Red had gotten herself into such a fix.

At least Red could be grateful for that. Now though, she had to suffer through another night of restlessness. Another night of rebuke.

And anticipation.

Michael finished pounding the fence post into the hard ground before he stood and wiped his brow, his gaze on the road leading to his house.

He'd chosen to work on the fence close to the house today, just in case the schoolmarm kept her word. He wasn't holding out much that she would, but even so, his eyes kept darting down the vacant road.

For Caroline's sake he hoped she showed. His daughter had been abuzz ever since Miss Wilde declared she was going to visit. This morning, before he'd headed out, she'd forced Michael to help her prepare a few things just in case.

On the other hand, he hoped she stayed away. Miss

Wilde was trouble; he felt it in his blood. He still couldn't believe he hadn't flat out put her in her place when she'd declared she would visit today.

Her challenge had stunned him. He hadn't been prepared for it. Hadn't had time to respond. A drastic difference from his response—and the sound defeat she'd suffered—on her first visit.

This time, there was no doubt she'd gotten the best of him. Left him with his mouth open, as she'd coolly hightailed it. He'd almost smiled afterward. He almost smiled now. His fear that Caroline was going to get hurt if Miss Wilde didn't keep her promise held him back, though.

What would he do if she failed to show?

If he had to console his daughter, there would be hell to pay. He might even bring it to the school committee's attention. It couldn't be good to have a teacher who didn't follow through on her word.

He glanced up at the sky, noting the sun had already peaked and was heading west. It was midday and there was still no sign of her.

He wiped his brow again, more from worry than from perspiration. The temperature couldn't have hit forty today and clouds were hovering about the Rockies, signaling snow. He hadn't lived in the area long enough to experience a Colorado snowstorm yet, but he'd lived through enough in the east, before the move, to know what to expect. Maybe she'd decided the weather was going to hit and she had no way to tell him. He hoped not—for Caroline's sake.

His jaw tightening, he turned his attention back to the fence, turned his back to the road, and decided he'd given Miss Wilde enough of his attention. Which just confirmed his assessment about her; she was trouble.

He'd no sooner raised his hammer to a new post before he heard the faint rattle of harness and a feminine giggle.

He peered over his shoulder to see her buggy, dust flying behind her, moving along the road. A child sat next to her and laughed again.

Michael's stomach quivered and his heart sped up.

He watched the buggy approach the house, watched Miss Wilde reenter his life. Cursing himself for a fool, he dropped his hammer and headed for the house.

Red took a deep breath as the ranch house came into view. Beside her, Sarah kept up a steady stream of conversation, relaying how her cousin, Tommy, had tangled with a skunk on Monday. Aunt June had made Tommy sleep in the barn for two nights and Uncle Luke had had to scrub Tommy raw before the smell went away.

Red laughed at Sarah's telling and tried to quell her nerves. She just needed to get through the next hour. One hour. Then she'd never set herself up to tangle with Michael Wisdom again.

"Are we here?" Sarah asked as they pulled up to the house.

"This is the place," Red told her. She forced a smile while Sarah bounced on the seat and layers of yellow ruffles swished around her.

The front door opened and Caroline ran out onto the porch.

"Good afternoon, Caroline," Red called. The child also wore a dress that had lots of ruffles. It was soft blue and had lace cuffs and a collar. Even her socks had lace edging and were stark white above her shiny black, high-top, flat-heeled boots. She had obviously dressed for the occasion.

Red brought the buggy to a halt and Sarah stood up in the seat. "Good afternoon, Caroline," she mimicked Red.

"Good afternoon," Caroline replied. Red saw her squeeze her hands and quiver excitedly.

Red exited the buggy, determined not to scan the area for signs of Caroline's father. She moved around to help Sarah down, then watched as Sarah ran up the porch steps. She was several inches shorter than Caroline but she clasped Caroline's hands in her own.

"Oh, Caroline, I'm so glad to meet you!" Sarah exclaimed.

Caroline's smile was radiant. "I have a new doll. Her name is Beth. Would you like to meet her?"

Sarah nodded broadly and the two girls ran inside the house together.

In that moment, Red was glad she'd come. Seeing

the happiness both girls shared was reward enough for her sacrifice.

She stood alone a moment and collected herself. Looking west—just to check on the weather—she could feel the cool breeze against her face, see the wind rustling the tall brown grasses, stirring the landscape of rolling hills and plains. Storm clouds continued to obscure the mountain peaks, but they remained far away, posing no immediate threat.

Neither, it would seem, did Mr. Wisdom. Of course, he could be in the house. He was maintaining his rudeness by staying inside instead of greeting her.

Odds were, though, he'd made himself scarce; he was out tending cattle or something, which was fine with her. The less she saw of him, the better. She was here for Caroline and Sarah, no one else.

She entered the house with that thought firmly planted and was immediately struck by the echo her boots made. Glancing around, she noted the barren interior. The entry was wide, with a polished hardwood floor and subtly papered walls, but no hall tree, coat rack, pictures or bric–a–brac graced the area. The entry led directly into a square medium–sized parlor void of furnishings except for a multi–colored yarn rug on the hardwood floor.

Following two very excited voices, Red moved down the hollow corridor and peered inside a dining room, complete with chandelier and papered walls in greens and blues but with a small out–of–place rough–hewn table and two chairs. Sarah and Caroline sat on their knees in the chairs, Caroline's doll, Beth, beside her. In stark contrast to the table, a rose patterned china tea set rested on the surface, a crystal platter laden with tea-cakes beside it. The scent of brewed tea filled the air.

"Look, Aunt Meredith," Sarah exclaimed. "Caroline and her papa made us a tea party."

And her papa?

Red dismissed that information, certain Sarah was mistaken. Mr. Wisdom might have helped Caroline set out the tea set, but she couldn't fathom his efforts going further. "How nice," she smiled and watched Caroline struggle to lift the pot filled with tea and carefully pour it into Sarah's cup.

"Sarah, you can add the sugar," Caroline said, her tongue touching her lip as she concentrated. "Miss Wilde, would you like some tea?"

Only then did Red see her own place. She had a setting with a teacup and saucer but no chair to sit in. "Why I'd love some, Caroline, thank you." She removed her cloak, silently helped Sarah from hers, and searched the room for a place to store them.

"I'll take those," she heard then.

Her stomach lurched and she spun to see Michael standing in the doorway.

"Papa!" Caroline cried. "My new friend is here, Papa. I told you Miss Wilde would remember. See, she wasn't too busy."

"Yes," Michael replied. His gaze settled on Red's and she felt her face heat up.

"T–this is Sarah Caulder," she managed. She extended the coats his way, making certain their hands didn't touch. As soon as her arms were empty she moved closer to Sarah.

"Hello," Sarah greeted.

Michael nodded. Then he backed out of the door.

Red exhaled, even as she wondered if he planned to return. She hadn't heard him arrive. Dear Lord, his voice had made her stomach do somersaults and her skin tingle clear down to her toes.

Shaking still, she tried to refocus on the girls and not give consideration to where he had gone.

"Now for our cakes," Caroline said after she'd filled Red's cup and set the heavy pot down. "They're special cakes. My grandmamma used to make them for Daniel and me. That's my brother." Caroline lifted the tray but had to set it back down before the weight of it caused her to drop it.

Red circled the table and lifted it for her, glad for the diversion. "They look delicious, Caroline," she commented. She wanted to ask who had made them, but she didn't dare.

She nearly dropped the platter herself when Caroline said, "My papa and me made them this time 'cause my grandmamma doesn't live by us anymore."

Red tried to smile, but surely she'd heard wrong. She

extended the tray to Sarah who looked long and hard at the different sized and shaped tarts. Sarah finally settled on a sugarcoated concoction that oozed custard.

"I like the apple one," Caroline said when presented the platter for inspection. She snatched one up.

Red set the platter down and examined the contents herself before settling on a small multi-layered pastry that had a dollop of heavy cream on top. She didn't believe for a moment that Michael had prepared the cakes. Perhaps he'd bought them from Amelia Garvey, the owner of Ruley's restaurant.

Unless . . . she bit into hers, hoping it tasted like lard. To her surprise, it was as light and fluffy as it looked, and very tasty.

"Hmmm," Sarah said as she took a bite of her own cake. Custard dripped down her chin and she licked it away.

"Try your tea," Caroline encouraged. It was impossible to miss her eagerness. She so wanted her tea party to be a success.

"It's all delicious," Red told her. Truthfully. But how? The child could not have put everything together herself. And Red had not heard anything about Michael hiring a woman to cook and clean.

"Want to see my room?" Caroline asked a moment later. "I don't have it pretty like our other house but Papa said we would work on that soon." Sarah nodded and before Red knew it, the girls had run off.

Red walked to the doorway to watch them disappear

up a staircase. Before their footsteps faded, she heard another set beside her.

"Hope the tea wasn't too strong," Michael said, stopping before her. "Caroline made me brew it hours ago. Just in case you arrived early."

Red backed up a pace. He was being polite again. But at any moment his demeanor could change and she wasn't going to be in the line of fire.

Nevertheless, she smiled, touched by his words. "The tea was fine, thank you. Not too strong at all." Had he really prepared it? She tried to peer through the door into the kitchen to see if it was a disaster, but the only area she was able to see was a clean cupboard and washbasin.

He skirted by her into the dining room. Red felt a warm breeze as he passed, breathed in his scent of dirt and mustiness and water and soap. He'd been working, she concluded. Had he come inside and washed up when he saw her arrive?

More confusion sidled through her. That, and a tremor deep in her stomach. Who was this man? And why did he rattle her so?

She pivoted back into the dining room to face him.

"Please have a seat," he said, taking Caroline's. "You're welcome to finish your tea. Caroline has a list of things she was determined to share with your cousin. It's grown every day, so they'll be awhile."

Red wanted to tell him that sharing was typical of little girls, but nothing about this situation was typical, so she kept quiet and complied with his offer, sitting opposite him in the chair Sarah had vacated. The tea helped calm her, even if her hands continued to shake.

"I guess you know I didn't think you'd come here today," Michael said then and Red's nerves stood on end.

"Caroline implied as much." She pressed the cup to her lips.

"The last couple of days," he went on. "Well, she's been as excited as I've ever seen her. I didn't want her to be disappointed."

"I understand."

"Probably not. She's been disappointed a lot in her young life." He fingered the flower on the teacup as if reflecting. "She hasn't had this tea set out since we moved. Hasn't used it since her mother and older brother died. She used to badger Daniel into having tea parties with her. He was five years older than her. She'd plead and plead with him until he gave in."

His declaration had Red holding her breath. "Daniel must have been a good brother. And the tea set is lovely," she replied, gazing at the rose–patterned flowers. "I hope Caroline will want to keep it out now." She glanced around at the bare walls. "It helps warm up the room."

She immediately regretted her words. He was sharing significant elements of his life and she was casting judgment. "I mean . . . that is—"

He cleared his throat, freezing her in place.

"Guess so," he agreed. If he was going to say more,

the girls prevented him from doing so when they came bounding into the room. Giggling and screeching, they raced around the table before Caroline halted in front of her father. "Papa, can I show Miss Wilde and Sarah my pond? Please?"

Michael's shoulders stiffened. "Not this time, Caroline. We're not prepared for a long walk today."

Caroline's face fell. "But I want to show Sarah." She turned to Sarah, her eyes shining. "Papa said the pond in back of our house was my pond. He named it Buttercup Pond, after me. We went swimming in it when it was warm. And he's gonna let me skate on the ice when it freezes. I used to skate with my brother before we came here. My mama always said she'd skate with us too, but she never did; Daniel would get mad."

"Caroline, that's enough," Michael cautioned.

"Is the water frozen yet, Papa?"

"Not yet," he replied. "Remember I told you it has to snow a few times before that happens." The chair scraped and he stood, clearly agitated.

Caroline grabbed Sarah's hand, oblivious. "Uh-huh. Seven times, Papa said. After it's snowed seven times the water will freeze and then we can skate. You can come skating too, Sarah. It's fun."

Sarah nodded excitedly, although Red was sure the child didn't know the first thing about ice–skating. It was still considered an eastern activity.

"I'm sure Sarah will be able to join you when the ice is ready," Red told Caroline.

"You too, Miss Wilde? Will you come skating too?"

Red considered. "I suppose. I skated many times while growing up in New York." She stood then, pretending not to notice the perplexed furrow of Michael's brow. He had probably thought she had been born in Colorado. "But we'll leave skating for another day. Right now, Sarah and I best be going."

Both girls moaned, so Red added, "I think the weather will turn soon, and I promised I'd have Sarah home by mid–afternoon."

Caroline was the first to protest. She ran to Red and clung to her skirts, peering up at her. "But we haven't braided my hair yet," she complained. "Please, can't you stay for a little while longer?"

Red rubbed Caroline's back while warring with herself over whether she should stay or leave. In the end she knew she had to leave. "I wish we had more time, sweetheart. It'll have to wait until our next visit."

"Next visit?"

Red realized her mistake as soon as Caroline smiled. She had promised herself there would be no next visit. "Well I didn't exactly mean . . ." She looked at Michael, imploring him to intervene.

The faint lifting at the sides of his mouth, just enough to ease his scowl, signaled her he wasn't going to. But why? He'd made it plain he didn't want Red interfering in his daughter's life.

"Papa, can they come back?" The girl jumped up and down excitedly.

"If they want to, Caroline," he replied, much to Red's surprise and consternation.

"Tomorrow? Can we skate on my pond tomorrow?"

"The pond won't freeze over for awhile, Caroline. Weeks yet."

"How long before it snows seven times?"

"Weeks, Buttercup."

It was clear she didn't understand the concept of time. No child her age did. Red patted her shoulder. "Besides, we have church tomorrow. And school all next week. But . . . soon," she compromised.

"I want to go to church," Caroline cried. She turned to her father. "Can we go to church, Papa? Please? We used to go all the time before Mama and Daniel died. And since you won't let me go to school, I want to go to church." Caroline looked on the verge of tears and Red bit her lip, worried she'd started a situation.

Luckily, Michael knelt down in front of his daughter to address her. He gently cupped her upper arms in his large hands and though Red could tell he was agitated himself, he said, "We'll see. Let me give it some thought. For now you need to say good–bye to Miss Wilde and Sarah, and thank them for coming. They won't want to come back if you carry on so."

Caroline's shoulders sagged but she sniffed and rubbed her eyes. Red had such an urge to comfort her, tell her what she wanted to hear. But her impulsiveness had gotten her in too much trouble already, so she clamped her mouth shut and kept it that way. Despite

the pain she saw in Caroline, she couldn't commit anything else to the child. She just couldn't. Not when
there was such—what? Animosity? Attraction? Strain,
she decided, between her and Caroline's father.

"Can you tell Caroline thank you, Sarah?" she managed. When Sarah had complied, Red added, "We had
a wonderful time, Caroline. You are an excellent hostess. I wish I could make pastries like yours."

"They aren't so hard. They just take time. I'll give
you the recipes," Michael said.

Red felt her jaw drop. "*You* made them?"

When one side of his face lifted in a whisker-
shadowed grin she had to brace herself with a hand to
the wall. The sight transformed his face, softening his
hard eyes, causing slivers of gold to shimmer around
the irises.

It nearly knocked Red off her feet.

"You okay?"

She blinked. "I find it difficult to believe you made
those pastries," she covered.

"Papa makes lots of things. He had to 'cause Mama
didn't know how."

His smile faded but he shrugged and put his arm
around Caroline's shoulders. "I learned out of necessi-
ty. Guess I could have stuck with bread and water but
that didn't seem appealing. And Daniel and Caroline
would have never stopped complaining."

Red could only nod. Michael Wisdom was more than

confusing. She moved through the door, glad when a stiff breeze blew across her face.

"When will you come back?" Caroline pressed from behind her.

"I'll look at my schedule," she answered, planting one foot in front of the other. Dry, dead leaves crunched beneath her feet as she crossed the yard to her buggy.

"Maybe we'll see you in church," Sarah offered. "If your pa thinks about it."

Church would be a good place for both father and daughter, Red decided. *Please Lord, I'm in way over my head with these two. But you aren't. Help Mr. Wisdom realize church would be a good place for him and his daughter. That way Caroline can make the friends she needs and I'll be off the hook.*

"I'll help you up," she heard to her left. Before her arrival, she had decided that if he offered his assistance in any way, she'd tell him she didn't need it. But her anger had subsided a long time ago. She'd learned so much about him. Too much. Now she couldn't find the words to rebuff him. Instead, she braced herself for his touch as he wrapped his hand around her arm. As expected, she found it warm, gentle, strong.

She took a steadying breath. Then, after she was seated and his hand slipped away, she felt a sudden and profound loneliness. Her emotions were absurd, she told herself. What was wrong with her? One minute she was furious with the man, the next breathless.

She had to put an end to this. "Caroline, Mr. Wisdom," she said. "Thank you for the hospitality. Sarah and I had a wonderful time."

"Good-bye, Sarah, Miss Wilde," Caroline shouted, recovered somewhat from her disappointment. "I can't wait to go skating on my pond with you."

"Good-bye, Caroline." Sarah waved as Red turned the buggy and hurried Honey onto the road.

She was halfway to the Caulder's ranch before she breathed again. Relief sidled through her. Finally. She'd done what she'd intended, she concluded. She'd made Caroline happy, introduced her to a new friend, kept her word, surprised Michael in the process, and now it was over. Thank goodness.

It would be up to Caroline now to press her father for more, and up to Red to forget the Wisdoms altogether. Forget how Caroline had worked so hard to please her, how her eyes sparkled when she was happy, how much she needed a woman in her life. Forget how Michael's touch set her to trembling, how his scent made her mouth water, how his smile nearly toppled her.

She had no choice but to forget. And yet the thought of their loss made her weep inside.

They were a pair, father and daughter. She was moody, a tad spoiled and needing more than Red could offer. He was fickle, ornery and as complicated as any man she'd ever met. She'd do well to remember that.

Chapter Four

"And then Red told me that little Caroline was a gracious hostess. She said her manners would have even satisfied my mother," Madeline Graham announced.

"Well, quite nearly," Red interjected, remembering how strict Maddie's mother could be. She gazed at her dark–haired sister, Kit, and then at her housemate. This Sunday morning the three ladies were on their way to church with Kit's husband, Sam, driving their carriage. Maddie had been Kit's best friend in finishing school. She'd followed Kit and Sam to Colorado after her parents had drowned at sea. An exuberant tall and thin woman, she had wanted to know everything about Red's visit to the Wisdoms' the moment Red had returned home. Now Maddie was relating to Kit the details Red had shared with her. She didn't know that Red had kept most of the details of her visit to herself.

"Your mother? The most etiquette-prone woman in New York?" Kit mused. Her vivid blue eyes sparkled, the soft yellow of her dress enhancing their hue. "Caroline must be some little girl."

"She's very bright," Red agreed, smiling at the thought of Caroline. She smoothed the lace cuffs of her starched white blouse beneath her mint green jacket and matching skirt. "She was trying hard to please Sarah and I."

"It sounds as if both girls had a wonderful time. It was good of you to arrange for them to meet, Red."

Red didn't want any praise. She knew her reasons were far less honorable than her sister gave her credit for. But she held her tongue. What was done was done. Much to her relief.

"What have you heard about Caroline's father, Sam?" Kit asked her husband with an elbowed nudge to his ribs. "Do you know how his wife and son lost their lives?"

"I've only seen Wisdom around town on a few occasions, said hello a couple of times, but we've never had a lengthy conversation," Sam replied as Red nonchalantly slid forward in her seat to hear her brother–in–law's reply. She told herself it was only natural for her to be curious. But Sam's response wasn't at all satisfying.

"I've heard he's a carpenter by trade," Sam went on

and Red perked up. "A few of the men in town questioned him when he arrived to claim Peter's ranch. He said he owned an equal share with his brother but because Peter had never mentioned that or him to anyone, some were suspicious."

Red remembered as much. But then, she'd heard, he'd produced the deed showing both his and Peter's name on it.

"Why did he fire all his help? That was rather strange," Kit said.

"Dortch and Sheriff Moss said he didn't trust them. Could be that he needed time alone if what Red heard was true. That he lost his wife and son. I remember hearing he was from Pennsylvania."

Caroline had said the family ice–skated in the winter so Pennsylvania made sense. The weather was as cold there as it was in New York.

"That's all?" Maddie asked, prodding Sam further.

Sam shrugged. "Guess so. I think he's proven he keeps to himself."

Red couldn't have agreed more, though she kept that opinion to herself. Sam had deepened her curiosity though, if what he said about Michael being a carpenter was true. Why, then, hadn't there been any furniture in the house except for the unsightly table with its splintery surface and wobbly legs? Had he left it all behind? Did Caroline have a bed upstairs in her room? Red suddenly wanted to ask Sarah if she'd seen one.

"Well, we've all been in a similar situation in our

lives, so we can't fault Mr. Wisdom for wanting his privacy," Kit said. "After Zachary's death I felt lost. Maddie, you felt the same way when you got the news about your parents drowning. And Sam, you too, when your sister died."

"I sure did," Sam agreed.

"Maybe Mr. Wisdom needed a fresh start after his wife and son died," Maddie added. "Like the rest of us." She sighed in reflection. "His was a terrible loss."

Kit placed a protective hand on her swelling stomach and nodded.

Sam covered his wife's hand. "I couldn't imagine losing you and the child growing inside you," he said.

Kit smiled as tears filled her eyes. Red heard Maddie sniff and she blinked away her own tears. Then Sam was clearing his throat. "There's the clan," he said and nodded towards the church where April and Will, May and Travis, and June and Luke stood in a group on the lawn. Sarah and her cousins—June's son Tommy, and May's son Matthew—were running in circles around their parents' legs while April held her toddler son, Caleb.

April waved as she saw the carriage approach.

With a relieved sigh, the subject of Michael, if not her thoughts of him, fell away. She followed Kit and Sam and Maddie to the others in front of the church.

"I heard about Tommy's run–in with the skunk," Kit said to June, which started another conversation. For the next several minutes everyone chatted about their week. Red heard that June was finally over her morning sickness, that Luke had landed another large contract with the city of Denver to supply more street lamps, and that Travis had quarantined the Hollis family who were all down with influenza. May was busy nursing a bear cub whose mom had died, and April and Will were getting ready to enter one of their horses in a race called the Kentucky Derby.

When asked, Red talked about this year's plans for the Christmas pageant but said nothing about her encounters with the Wisdoms.

With the banter running on high, she'd nearly managed to put Michael from her mind when Sarah called out, "Caroline!"

Stunned, Red whirled to see Caroline hurrying across the grass. Michael wasn't far behind.

Her heart lurched. She was more than surprised to see them. Caroline was grinning from ear to ear. The expression on Michael's face was just the opposite. His hat was nowhere to be found. His hair had been slicked back and was still damp. One lock fell over his forehead, adding to his appeal. His jaw was freshly shaven, his gaze hesitant, and he wore ironed slacks, a crisp white shirt, and a dark jacket.

"Caroline! You came to church!" Sarah exclaimed as Red fought to stay upright. "Mama, this is my new friend."

"My papa thought about it and said we could come," Caroline replied. Brightness radiated around her. She was far different from the girl Red had met back in July. She stepped closer to Red and wrapped her arms around Red's skirt.

Red knelt down to Caroline's height, welcoming the distraction. "It's good to see you, Caroline," she said.

"I didn't give up talking to Papa until he changed his mind," she whispered. "That was good, wasn't it?"

"Yes, sweetheart. It was." Red fought away a grin, the child's innocence refreshing.

"Sorry for the interruption," Michael said then.

Red's anxiety returned. She rose as he arrived.

"No need to apologize," Will answered, extending his hand. "Will Caulder and my wife April," he introduced. "I guess our daughters became friends yesterday."

"Michael," Luke said. "Good to see you again. Your horses' shoes holding up?"

"I never did thank you for bringing Trip to my office," Travis added.

Caroline spun back to Sarah and the girls raced away hand in hand, giving Red the opportunity to quietly retreat while Michael shook hands and met the rest of her family.

It was Kit who caught up to her when she was about to enter the church alone. Her sister slid an arm around Red's and whispered, "Can you believe we were just talking about Mr. Wisdom? Funny how things like that happen. Caroline does seem to be a sweet child. I can tell you adore her. But you didn't tell me her father was gorgeous. Gorgeous and a widower."

Red slanted Kit a look. "He's the most unavailable widower I've ever met," she told her.

"Is he? Ghosts from the past?" Kit questioned.

"Among other things." Michael had more flaws than her old battered desk at school. The one Elias Burton didn't have any funds to replace.

Kit pulled Red to a halt in the aisle as parishioners moved around them. "I remember how I despised Sam when he came to arrest me. Then how angry I was when I found out he wasn't arresting me at all but taking me back so he could collect a bounty. And I wasn't any better off having been married to a man who never loved me. I had some deep wounds from Zachary's rejection. You think we didn't have to do some changing? It can happen, Meredith."

Red knew just how much adversity her sister had been through. She had been haunted by the death of her first husband, and believed she'd contributed to his death. She'd also been accused of his murder by Sam, no less, who had nearly led her into the real killer's hands.

But this was different. "I wouldn't be interested in Mr. Wisdom even if he did change," she told her sister and herself. He was still in love with his deceased wife. That was obvious. Honorable and obvious. And Red had no inclination to interfere with that memory. Even if it was possible, even if Michael could get over the past, Red was more than certain he wouldn't be interested in her.

She hugged her sister and continued up the aisle,

greeting Pastor Johnson as he made his way to the door to welcome the rest of the worshipers. She slipped into one of the pews and sat down, Kit beside her. Maddie and Sam arrived a few moments later and Red scooted over so Maddie could sit between her and Kit.

Rattled by her conversation with her sister and by seeing Michael only moments ago, she fought for recovery. All the while she wondered if he intended to stay for service or was just dropping Caroline off. And if he'd eaten the leftover pastries he'd made or tossed them outside for the birds. Or if he'd washed the tea set and put it away or left it on the table to brighten the room. Or if he planned to have his furniture—furniture he'd possibly made with his own hands—ever shipped from Pennsylvania.

Exhaustion set in, making Red weary. She'd tried so hard not to think about him. And she'd been certain she was winning.

Until he decided to bring his daughter to church.

She didn't want to complain. Hadn't she prayed for just that? Yes, she had. Repeatedly last night and again this morning before she'd swung her legs out of bed.

But had she really thought he'd give in? No, she hadn't. She was still finding it difficult to believe.

Worse, she didn't want to think about him. Not last night, nor this morning, or now. Especially now. These few hours were reserved for God. She was so busy all the time she rarely had time for her Maker. She sometimes thought busyness was the greatest sin of all.

But how could she forget about him when suddenly

Caroline was tapping her on her shoulder, waving to her, and Red was realizing that Caroline and Michael were sitting right behind her? How could she forget when the swirl of air he created caused her to catch a slight whiff of his distinctive scent? It was impossible to forget him when she heard his smooth voice hesitantly singing *The Old Rugged Cross.* It became harder when Pastor Johnson quoted Solomon's words from the seventh chapter of Ecclesiastes.

"Consider the work of God . . . for in the day of prosperity be happy, but in the day of adversity consider— God has made the one as well as the other."

Could it be mere coincidence that Michael was in church for such a message? Was it possible that God had Pastor Johnson speak on the topic Michael needed to hear most?

She had told him that she believed everything happened for a reason. But had she really believed it?

As staggered as she was, the coincidences were enough to make her reflect on Kit's words about how people could change, but she was more than glad when services ended and she could escape outside.

She purposely walked to the far side of the lawn and struck up a conversation with Wanda Etherton while she waited for the rest of the family to assemble for the short drive to April and Will's for their ritual Sunday supper get–together. She hoped amid all the bustling activity that usually accompanied their large gathering, she would finally find some peace of mind.

Michael, she couldn't help but notice, finally exited the church as well, pausing at the door to shake Pastor Johnson's extended hand as Caroline and Sarah bounded down the steps in front of him. And then, much to her annoyance, Will was shaking Michael's hand again and asking Michael to join the family for supper. Worse, Michael was accepting the invitation. Sarah and Caroline jumped up and down with joy.

For Red, it was all too much. She politely excused herself from Wanda's company and headed for Sam's carriage.

"Not to your liking?" Kit asked, catching up to her and wrapping her arm around Red's once more.

"What do you mean?" Red asked, feigning ignorance. "Pastor Johnson's message was inspiring as always. Of course I liked it."

"You know very well that's not what I'm talking about," Kit told her. She tucked a strand of Red's hair back into the pale green hat she wore. "I'm talking about Mr. Wisdom joining the family for supper."

"Is he? How wonderful for Caroline," Red managed.

"This is harder on you than I thought," Kit said. She paused midstep and stared at Red. "If you're attracted to him, you should be excited. Are you going to be all right?"

"I'm not attracted to Mr. Wisdom. I'm fine," Red lied, knowing the afternoon would be no easier for her than the morning.

*   *   *

She heard his laugh for the first time, a reaction to something Sam said while they all sat at April's long table, eating her tender chicken and plump dumplings. She learned he had plans to expand his cattle herd in the spring and was very interested in April's success in breeding racehorses.

Before the meal, he was ever attentive to Caroline, who continued to bloom while playing with the rest of the children, and he had a knack for whittling—which made sense if he was a carpenter—that rivaled Luke's, so they carved Tommy and Matthew new slingshots.

In general, she managed to steer clear of Michael most of the day by taking a walk to view an eagle May had healed and released, and by staying in the kitchen. But even as she steered clear of him, she was aware of his every move. It was as if she were attuned to everything about him.

Have mercy, she finally cried silently and looked heavenward. *I know this isn't the man for me. You wouldn't be so cruel. So why am I so drawn to him? Can't you do something about this?*

She'd never been one to pray gently. Sometimes she was a bit concerned about her irreverence. But she also knew God had a sense of humor—He must to have put up with her all these years—so she didn't worry too much. She was just a human after all.

She managed to blend into the background after her prayer. She thought she'd done a good job too until Caroline ruined her efforts.

"Papa, look how pretty Miss Red made me!" she'd shouted to Michael after Red had braided her hair. "She borrowed a ribbon from Sarah. Look. It's pink. Didn't Miss Red make me pretty?" She ran into the living room where the men were seated and enjoying coffee and May's plum pie.

"Miss who?" Red heard him say from around the corner in the kitchen. She reached for a towel and proceeded to wipe a plate dry, pretending not to listen. Pretending the way she had all day.

"Miss Red. You know, Miss Meredith," Caroline replied loudly. "Didn't you know everyone calls her that? I just learned too, so it's all right if you didn't."

She could almost feel Michael's gaze shift her way. She'd discarded her heavy green jacket and rolled up her sleeves hours ago and now his stare burned into her back. She forced herself to breathe and continued to dry the plate in counter–clockwise fashion while she waited for his reply. Surely he would confirm his daughter's assessment that she looked pretty. And maybe he would add that Miss Red had a talent for braiding.

When he said, "You look just like your mother did when her hair was braided," her hand froze on the plate. She could feel the blood drain from her face.

"Here, let me take that."

She looked down at the plate she held in a death grip and then at her sister. What she saw was pity in Kit's eyes. April, May, June, and Maddie stood silently with the same expression on their faces.

A burst of panic rushed through Red's veins. Had they all guessed what she was feeling? "I . . . my, it's warm in here. I think I'll get some air." Her legs felt wobbly as, her chin high, she gave the plate to Kit and walked to the front door. She refused to look in the direction of the men as she went.

Kit was right behind her, having handed the plate to Maddie. When they were alone on the porch, she said, "Men can be insensitive dolts."

The brisk evening breeze whipped Red's skirts and chilled her cheeks but gave her the air she needed. She blinked rapidly, fighting away moisture that was pooling in her eyes. "I don't know what you mean," she said and paced the porch.

"Yes you do," Kit countered. "Stop trying to pretend with me. It isn't every day I see my sister all aflutter over a man. And I know all about that feeling."

Red drew in a shaky breath. "This is all so ridiculous. Tell me I haven't been fluttering all day. I've tried very hard not to . . . you know . . . flutter. Is it that apparent? I don't even like the man. He's hardheaded and arrogant and—"

"—and just like the rest of the men in this family," April interjected. She stepped outside to join Red and Kit. Maddie, June, and May were right behind her.

Red groaned. "He's very much in love with his wife,

and that's all there is to it," she told them. "Even if he weren't, he's not interested in me. Maybe he finds Maddie attractive. She's just as husbandless as I am. Why aren't you interested in what she thinks of the man?"

"He's not Madeline's type," June suggested.

"It's not the same," May claimed.

"The sparks between you two can't be missed," April added.

Sparks? Red sighed.

"We're just sorry to see you so upset." Kit took Red's hands into her own.

"I wouldn't be if the man would just go away," Red admitted. "He . . . he . . . he's such a pest."

"Aren't they all," April jested and everyone laughed.

"Listen, darling," Maddie chimed in. "He's as handsome a man as I've ever seen and if I had met him first you might have some competition on your hands. But since I didn't and you don't, I say you've got everything it takes to make his wife's memory just that; a memory."

Red just stared at her cousins and sister as they nodded in agreement.

"I'm not going to compete with her," she said. "He loves her too much."

"And if he didn't?" Kit asked.

"I don't know," Red replied. She didn't want to know. The very idea was terrifying. "It isn't an issue because he does. You heard what he said to Caroline. He says things like that all the time.

"Please. I hear all of you and love you for your concern but there is nothing to this. It's time to go home. Kit, please see if Sam's ready to leave. I still have class to prepare for tonight."

Michael tucked Caroline into her bed and blew out the candle, watching as the moonlight settled over her cherubic features. She'd chattered all the way home, halfway up the stairs, and had finally yawned herself into silence. Only after he'd rocked her in his arms awhile had she found sleep. Then he'd settled her into bed.

Her hair was still all twisted into a braid over her shoulder, wispy curls clinging to her sweet face and neck. He stifled an urge to smooth them away from her brow. He'd told her she looked like her mama, but the real truth was, she didn't. She had the look of her grandmamma, Michael's mother, if anyone. Her other grandmother, Claire's mother, and Claire, had features that were more prominent, sculpted, rather than softly round.

He'd told Caroline differently because that was his habit. He'd started when she'd told him about a year after Claire's death that she couldn't remember what her mama looked like anymore. He presumed that was because Claire had been absent from Caroline's life even before the fire had taken her away, but he had never slandered Claire in front of Caroline and he didn't plan on ever doing so. But since they'd never had a picture taken of their family—much to his regret now—he'd begun to tell Caroline she looked like her mother just so, when she looked in the mirror, she'd think she remembered.

He didn't regret the fib. But he shouldn't have fibbed today.

The day had gone smoother than he'd thought it would up until then. He'd made it through the church service without too much angst, even concentrating on the pastor's words a bit more than he'd thought he would. He'd made it through supper in the midst of Meredith Wilde's large family, laughed at a few things the men said and been able to relax in their presence. Then he'd made the mistake of commenting on Caroline's hair. Tension had seeped into the room like a thick fog. He'd watched as Meredith headed outside, as the other women followed her, and as the men turned their attention to their pie.

Red, Caroline had called her. And he'd been so taken aback.

The pet name fit her. Too well. He'd realized he didn't know much about her. The others did. They cared about her, shared her life, called her by her pet name, and . . . he'd felt excluded.

His reaction had been to lash out. He'd deliberately wanted to wound her. He hadn't missed his mark and everyone knew it.

The gathering had broken up soon thereafter and he'd felt like a dang fool ever since. He was sure none of them would ever be hospitable to him again. And whether he liked it or not, that mattered.

It shouldn't. It wouldn't have only a couple weeks ago. He rationalized that it mattered because of Caroline. And he rationalized that it mattered because he'd enjoyed the men's company and the ladies' cooking. He hadn't been part of such a friendly atmosphere in a long while.

But he knew it mattered most because of her.

Meredith Wilde.

Red.

Days later, she slipped into her seat behind the table at Amelia's Restaurant with a weary sigh. "Sorry I'm late," she told Maddie. "Not only has Trip Dawson made a new commitment to his studies, but he has so many questions, I've had to ask him to save them until after class."

"Don't fret over it," Madeline told her. "I've had plenty to keep me occupied." She took a sip of her white wine while Red smoothed the skirt of her powder blue dress, adjusted her linen napkin over her lap, and then sighed again.

Ever since Sunday, she had worked herself ragged. She'd completed enough lessons for the next two months, decided which children would play the roles of Mary, Joseph, the three wise men, and the shepherd boy in the pageant, and even come up with the idea of selling baked goods so she could purchase some of the supplies she needed. The only tasks she had left were to find a baby Jesus and convince a few friends and family members to help her bake.

Joining Maddie for supper was the first time she'd slowed down all week. Every Thursday, weather permitting, she and Maddie dined at Amelia's Restaurant. Maddie was a New Yorker through and through. She still craved the theaters, museums and restaurants New York offered. In Ruley, Amelia's was as close as it got. The food was well prepared, varied, Amelia was a gracious proprietress, and the atmosphere was lively. Red enjoyed splurging once a week.

Tonight was a welcome reprieve even though there was still snow on the ground from Monday's storm and the air was frigid. Everyone was saying that it felt like mid–January instead of the first of December. Red wondered if they were in for a long winter.

"And what kept you so busy?" she asked as she reached for the cup of tea Maddie had already procured for her. "I thought you had time to spare today."

Maddie swallowed more wine and set the glass down. "I received a letter today," she answered. "From Smith Weatherby. Do you remember him? Maybe not. Kit will. I can't wait to tell her about this. Smith and I, well, he was my unofficial intended while I was still in finishing school. I loved him and I thought he loved me."

"Maddie you've never told me any of this."

Maddie shrugged. "Probably because one night he announced to his parents, me and my parents, as well as a hundred guests at the Vandergard's ball, that he and Lucia Montgomery had eloped."

"You're not serious?"

"It's been five years." Maddie shook her head in reflection. "Before I left New York I heard that Lucia had died during childbirth. I don't know if the child lived.

"In his letter Smith says he wants to come visit me. In fact, based on the postmark, he's on his way. He left New York two days ago."

"Maddie."

"I can't believe it myself."

Red covered Maddie's hand with her own. "What reason does he give for wanting to see you?"

"That's the craziest thing of all. He hints that he wants to marry me. Here, let me read this to you." She pulled the letter from her reticule and scanned the page. "Although I know I have no right to ask for your forgiveness, dear Madeline, please consider that I've learned a hard lesson. I'll explain all the details upon my arrival. Until then, I ask that you think favorably of me and know that my feelings for you were never false. It is my fondest wish that we pick up where we left off, albeit with a different outcome." She set the letter aside. "I never expected this."

"Isn't that the strangest thing? After all this time, to get a letter like that," Amelia said as she approached the table. Maddie, Red surmised, must have already shared the news with her. Amelia placed a hand on her plump hip, her multi-colored plaid apron covering most of her cambric dress. "Are you both having the special? Tonight I've got my delicious Irish stew and peach cobbler."

Amelia winked after they'd ordered. "I'll wager our Maddie here is on the road to getting hitched soon. Mark my words."

Could that be possible? Red wondered with a slight twinge of fear. "You knew this man well?" she asked after Amelia walked away. She purposely lowered her voice, aware that the dining room was crowded and gossip would travel faster than a blizzard if the news leaked. "Why did he marry someone else?"

Maddie toyed with her wine glass. She looked pretty tonight in her fashionable print dress that gathered tight at the waist and had billowing long sleeves. Her dark hair, pulled into a swirling chignon, gave her a regal appearance. Red had always admired her soft blue eyes. "His father and mine were both colonels," she explained. "That's how we met. I was fourteen and Smith a year older. We were besotted the moment we saw each other at one of the military balls. We spent the entire summer together. We even talked about what we'd name our children while we lazed about during those sweltering summer days. When I was seventeen, we decided to wait until after my commencement ceremony to announce our engagement. Two months later, Smith made a very different announcement.

"Rumor spread that Lucia was with child but when a child failed to arrive, I concluded Smith must have wanted to marry her after all."

"Do you think she lied to Mr. Weatherby?"

"Many people did. My mother included. She was more furious than I that Smith had done such a thing. She and my father had already planned their tour of Europe and she tried to convince me to join them, but I decided to stay and face the shame. Of course, you know they drowned when their ship sank on the way home.

"Concerning Smith, I don't know what I think."

"This is astonishing. Are you going to receive him?"

Maddie pondered, the blue of her eyes brightening. "I haven't decided yet. Would you?"

Red knew she and Maddie were very different people and had very different opinions. She'd have probably torn the letter into bits and pieces, burned it, and slugged the man if he ever appeared at her door. Maddie, on the other hand, was more good-natured and better at forgetting past transgressions.

And Mr. Weatherby might truly be sincere. Did he deserve a second chance?

"If I thought he was genuinely repentant, I suppose I'd receive him," Red replied, knowing that was probably what Maddie wanted to hear. "At least you have a few weeks to decide."

"Yes. I'm sure he won't arrive until the new year. I must tell Kit. I'll visit her tomorrow, I think. She was just as stunned as everyone else when Smith eloped. She cried with me on many occasions in those first few weeks. Perhaps I'll have her receive him first. Then, if she approves, I'll give him the opportunity he wants."

"That's a good idea," Red concurred, but she didn't think Maddie heard her. Maddie, Red realized, was already lost in thoughts of Smith Weatherby. Men, it seemed, had a way of occupying one's thoughts. She had purposely overloaded herself with work so she wouldn't have time to dwell on the men plaguing her own life, but they persisted in tormenting her just the same.

Elias Burton was one of them. He'd arrived at the schoolhouse yesterday to ask her to reconsider joining him for supper. He'd worn a bowler hat over his white–blonde hair and a tailor–made suit. He looked debonair and cultured. His grandfather had relocated he and Elias after Elias' father took his own life when Elias was sixteen. His mother had died years earlier. Prior to that, the family had been prominent in Boston social circles, so the suicide was a scandal. Elias pretended he and the patriarch had moved west to attend the newly opened Colorado School of Mines but after his graduation, his interest in politics emerged.

Prompted by his grandfather, he was currently winding his way up that ladder, and Red had no doubt he'd succeed. He'd probably become governor one day.

As he had stood in the schoolroom waiting for her answer, Red had heard the voices of the town matrons declaring he was the most eligible catch around. But her decision hadn't wavered. She had never considered Elias to be a genuine person. And his pursuit of a political career made him even less desirable. She was outspoken when she had to be, true, but being in the limelight all her life held no appeal.

Besides, she didn't think it was proper for them to have anything other than a professional relationship. After all, he was, in principle, her superior. He governed her work, made decisions regarding her on behalf of the town. He'd already made it clear that he could fulfill her request for supplies if she'd give in to his demands and that he wouldn't if she refused.

His duplicity had made her decision easy. She'd stood by as he left in a huff. Ever since she'd wondered why he didn't turn his attention to other women in town that would jump at the chance to marry him. The fact that he might try to retaliate against her began to worry her, although she couldn't think of anything he could do to harm her.

That wasn't so where Michael Wisdom was concerned. He had already made her heart hurt.

She and Maddie ate their meal in contemplative silence, and Red concluded that Amelia was probably right. Smith Weatherby would come along and sweep Maddie off her feet, and Red would be left alone.

As much as she loathed self–pity, she began to fall

under its spell. Why was it that her sister and three cousins had all found decent, loving men and she hadn't? Kit was expecting her first child in the spring. June was due in February. Sam and Luke fretted over the two of them like they were as fragile as crystal. Now perhaps Maddie had found someone as well.

Would Red ever have a love like that? She'd all but given up finding the right man.

Except in her deepest heart of hearts.

It made her wonder if she should reconsider Elias' invitation. Of course, there was always Vernon Wilcott. The gold miner had offered her a swig of his home-made whiskey at last month's fall festival. And trapper Leonard Monarch had invited her to go raccoon hunting with him.

Did it matter anymore if she compromised her pride and self–respect by marrying someone she didn't love? Why, just braiding a little girl's hair had earned her a lashing.

"How was supper?" Amelia said, breaking into Red's thoughts.

"Excellent as always, Amelia," she answered even as she pushed most of the uneaten meal aside. She'd lost her appetite when Maddie had told her about her letter.

"See you next Thursday," Maddie added as she and Red rose from their chairs.

"You bettcha. I'll be whipping up a few New York specials in the coming weeks so I'll be ready when you and yer beau come in," Amelia replied.

Maddie's face colored. "Amelia, hush."

The plump woman only giggled.

"She's impossible."

"Impossible," Red smiled. Her own self–pity was already dissolving. She would be truly happy for Maddie if she decided Mr. Weatherby was worthy of her affections. And she'd continue to live alone rather than with a man she didn't care for.

She pushed on the door, ready to face life's trials once more, when she felt it give as someone tugged from outside. She was greeted by a burst of cold air and Michael. "Oh. Mr. Wisdom. Hello."

"Miss Wilde."

"Mr. Wisdom," Maddie said with a glance to Red. "It's a pleasure to see you again. What brings you out on such a cold night? In town on business or are you meeting someone for supper?"

Red returned Maddie's glance with an irritated look of her own. "Madeline, I'm sure whatever Mr. Wisdom is doing is none of our concern."

"Ma'am," Mr. Wisdom acknowledged. He removed his hat and smoothed his hair before replacing it on his head, seemingly just as uncomfortable as Red.

"Please forgive Miss Graham's forwardness," Red added. "Perhaps she had a bit too much wine with supper tonight. We were just on our way out. If you'll excuse us."

"Why, Meredith, I did nothing of the kind," Maddie exclaimed, pretending offense. "I was just curious is all. If Mr. Wisdom is dining alone he might enjoy some company. And I don't believe we are pressed for time. We could stay for dessert and join him." She raised her shapely eyebrows, the blue of her eyes twinkling with mischief.

Red felt her face grow hot. She glared at Maddie, unappreciatively. "I'm sure Mr. Wisdom has other plans, Madeline," she forced with a smile.

"Let's find out. Do you, sir?" Maddie asked before Red could stop her.

"Why, Mr. Wisdom, did you conclude your business already?" Amelia interrupted then. She strolled their way, preventing Red from wrapping her hands around Maddie's neck. "Let me get that pie for you now."

Amelia turned to Red and Maddie. "Mr. Wisdom promised Caroline he'd bring her a piece of my apple pie. Isn't that the sweetest thing?"

He'd been to Amelia's earlier? Why had she never seen him there? Or Caroline? And where was Caroline now? Red peered through the window to see if the girl was waiting in the wagon. Surely he wouldn't have left her alone. Or back at the ranch.

"For that precious daughter of yours I'll make it a whole pie," Amelia added with a big smile. "But you must promise to give a piece to Sarah. She's always had a hankering for my pie too."

"I'll do that," Mr. Wisdom said.

"Caroline is with Sarah?" Red asked before she could stop the flow of words.

"She's been there all day. The two girls have become inseparable."

Red felt a warm shifting inside.

"Thanks to you," he added, taking the pie Amelia presented him from behind the counter. "I . . . actually, I'm glad I ran into you." He paused and glanced at Maddie and Amelia.

Maddie quickly said, "Amelia dearest, I was wondering if you could show me that new stove of yours." She took the woman by the arm and escorted her into the kitchen.

Red wanted to call them back but stopped herself and took a deep breath.

"I was going to stop by the schoolhouse tomorrow to see you," Michael went on.

"To see me?" She knew she sounded surprised and she was.

"To see you," he repeated. He dusted the shoulders of his coat and only then did Red realize it must be snowing again. "I have something I'd like to discuss with you."

"To discuss." She scolded herself for repeating him. For sounding like a ninny.

"Would it be all right if I stopped by? After school, that is?"

She could only nod, sure she was making a fool of herself but unable to do anything about it.

"Fine." He tipped his hat. "Tomorrow then," he added before departing.

"My, my, my," Amelia cooed when she and Maddie rounded the corner they'd been hiding behind.

"That was interesting, wasn't it?" Maddie chimed in.

Red stared at the two women but could think of nothing to say.

"What do you suppose he wants to discuss?" Maddie went on.

"I can't wait to find out," Amelia answered.

"You two are impossible," Red told them both. But she wondered the very same thing. And the thought made her nerves skitter.

Trying to sleep was futile. She slid out of bed before dawn, tried to concentrate on the day's lessons, gave that up as well, and proceeded to iron every skirt in her wardrobe. She changed outfits three times before infuriation forced her from her room and the house.

The frigid morning air seeped into her bones on the drive into town, a white dusting of snow on the ground giving a prelude to colder weather.

The shimmering white scenery made her remember why she had fallen in love with the Rocky Mountain region; it calmed her mind and gave her something other than herself to think about.

Still, once class had been dismissed and Trip Dawson was the only student still in the room, Red felt jumpier than a cat with a piece of yarn.

"How are you coming with that equation, Trip?" she asked just to give herself a task. She was *not* going to wile away the time fretting over Michael Wisdom's visit.

"They're getting harder, Miss Meredith," the boy replied. He'd been studying relentlessly ever since the day he'd broken his arm. He still wore a splint but nothing had slowed him down. He was now beginning to surpass even Red's knowledge.

"You're doing very well," she encouraged. "Take your time with each one. No need to rush." She smiled along with him just before she heard the school door creak open.

Pivoting, she saw Michael and her heart thumped. "Mr. Wisdom," she managed. Her voice sounded strange to her ears. "Please come in, won't you? You remember Mr. Wisdom, don't you Trip? He assisted us when you fell."

"Yes, ma'am. Sir. I guess I never did thank you proper." Trip started to rise from his chair.

"Go on with your work, young man," Michael said. "It appears you're healing well."

Trip sat back down. "I'm studying hard. I want to be a doctor."

"You what?" Red gasped.

Trip stared up at her. "I guess I probably shouldn't have said so 'cause . . . because I'll probably never be smart enough. But I owe you and Doc Travis for making me want to try."

Red had to blink quickly. If Michael hadn't been there she'd have burst into tears and shouted to the angels. As it was, she fought down her excitement. She leaned close to the boy. "Don't you ever say you're not smart enough. Don't you ever let anyone tell you you aren't smart enough. If you want to be a doctor, you will be. Oh Trip, I'm so proud of you."

He shrugged his gangly shoulders but sniffed. "I best get this problem solved then, so I can learn the next one."

Red beamed inside. Trip wanted to be a doctor. There was nothing more rewarding for a teacher than to hear that a pupil was going to use the information she was teaching him to better himself. "You do that," she told him before she shifted to face Michael again. "I'm sure you can appreciate how wonderful Trip's news is."

"I can." Michael tipped his head. "Becoming a doctor is a fine ambition. I'm sure you'll do everything you can to make sure Mr. Dawson succeeds."

"Yes. Yes I will," Red replied. She moved a distance from Trip, watched Michael follow, then fell silent, her gaze sweeping over his features, studying his face. His hat was in his hand, his dark hair was mussed, and whiskers shaded his firm chin. She searched his deep brown eyes for some sign of why he'd come, but even if he didn't reveal any animosity, he didn't reveal any desire either.

He'd been working, she could tell, by the dirt clinging to his boots and dungarees. And when he rubbed his forehead she could see the thick calluses on his hands.

"You wish to discuss something with me?" she asked with a tilt of her chin.

"She's as relentless as her mama ever was," he began and Red felt a direct jab to her heart.

"Caroline?" she asked, determined not to show him that the mention of his wife had hurt her again. She wondered why she didn't just tell the man to leave her alone. Did he get enjoyment from her pain?

"When she wants something she doesn't let up," he replied.

"Caroline," she said again. A statement. No longer a question. The child did have a stubborn streak in her.

"What's worse, she's usually right," he added, and Red found herself paying more attention to his words. "Unlike her mama. She's eight and more adult than she ever was. And her pa besides."

"I'm not sure I understand what you're getting at," she admitted.

"I know. I'm not making much sense. Just hear me out." The collar of his flannel shirt flexed as his jaw tightened. "Caroline thinks you can teach her better than I can. I've thought about it and . . ." he glanced at Trip, ". . . I'm willing to agree with her. The thing is, I'm not ready . . . I don't want her . . . I won't allow her to come to school. Alone. And with the ranch and all . . . Well, I can't bring her until the day's work is done."

Red listened in stunned silence. "Are you asking me to work with Caroline after class?" she finally asked.

He sat down in one of the student's chairs, his bulk dwarfing the furniture. She sank into one nearby and watched the conflict in his eyes. And waited. If she was disappointed for thinking there might have been another reason for his visit, for daring to hope, allowing it to disrupt her routine, the real reason diluted her sorrow.

Leaving the chair, she gave him her back so she could regain her composure. Then she faced him again. "I'm here until four daily. Class is dismissed by two-thirty. I usually have one or two students stay for a bit of extra attention. Trip has decided to remain every afternoon."

She stepped a little farther away. "This month is very busy. We'll be practicing for the Christmas pageant as well. If those things disturb you, I can't help. If not, I'd be happy to work with Caroline and . . . and you can stay if you'd like."

He stared at her long and hard, making Red shiver. "It's an imposition."

"Not at all."

"Extra work for you."

"I won't deny that."

He placed his hands on the desk and pushed himself to his feet, his jaw still tight, his gaze still cold. "You take on too much as it is."

"And how would you know such a thing?" Her defenses rising, her brow furrowed, her own jaw locked, and she glared at him, refusing to cower beneath that powerful stare.

"Everyone calls you Red?" he asked then, in a gravelly voice that she felt clear to her bones.

Red blinked, drawn off guard. "Just m–my family."

He slowly strode to her then, paused, and much to Red's shock, he lifted a stray lock of her hair that had escaped its pins and fallen over her shoulder. He gently smoothed the blades between his finger and thumb while she held her breath.

"We'll be here on Monday," he said and left.

Chapter Five

On Friday, the fourth storm of the season blew in, dropping the temperature so that Michael declared winter would be long and hard.

Caroline sucked in her breath with excitement when she heard Papa's words. When he left later that morning, she watched at the window. He pulled his coat collar up over his ears, rubbed his hands together, and rode out to join Gavin, Hank, and John in their work. He wouldn't be long, she knew. He never left her for long. Sometimes he made her go with him when he knew he was going to work longer than he wanted. But today was too cold and he didn't want her outside, so he'd told her he'd be back soon.

That didn't leave her much time.

She waited until he'd disappeared over the rise, then

she ran up to her room, donned her coat and mittens, and hurried back downstairs.

She just wanted to look at her pond.

Winter had arrived. Papa said so. And since it had already snowed four times, she was sure the water was frozen. Any day now she would be able to invite Sarah and Miss Red over and they could skate on Buttercup Pond. And then maybe she would be able to remember Daniel better again. And Mama too. Papa had said that if they kept doing the things they always did, she would never forget. But she didn't do any of the things she had done in the old house, like follow Papa to the barn to watch him work, or Daniel to the river to watch him fish, or watch Mama make herself pretty. They didn't go to Grandmamma Wisdom's farm, or the mansion Mama used to live in, and so everything in her mind was going away except a few mental images of the day she and Daniel and Mama were supposed to go to the circus.

Mama had promised them that since she hadn't taken them skating the day before, but she changed her mind again and said she was going to a party instead. Daniel had been so mad; he had cried and screamed at her and told her she didn't love him. He ran away and never came back, and Mama turned black and cried too. Caroline had stood at Mama's door and Papa had stayed by Mama's side, and then she went away too.

Maybe if Caroline had taken her brother skating and to the circus without Mama he wouldn't have gone away. Maybe if she went skating at Buttercup's Pond, he'd come back. And Mama too, if she wasn't too busy.

And this time, Miss Red would be there and Sarah, and they would all be happy. The pond had to be ready soon. It had snowed four times now. Papa said it had to snow seven times.

Today she might tap her foot on the edge a bit to see if the water was frozen. But she wouldn't tell Papa. He might not like it, and there was already sadness in his eyes. She didn't remember what he looked like without the sadness. Maybe she'd remember that too.

She left the house, glanced up and down the landscape just in case he'd decided to come back, and then she raced around the side of the house and down the path.

Buttercup's Pond was waiting for her.

"Quiet everyone. Listen please. Trip, take your place beside Reba. I'll refer to you both as Joseph and Mary from now on. You three wise men, over here."

The hum of voices diminished as Red began to move the children into place Monday afternoon. Those who were playing the parts of oxen, sheep, cows, mules and camels had already been dismissed. Today she just wanted to work with the children who had more substantial roles so she could better visualize the scene that would be set up in the town square.

As always, the mayor and sheriff were returning as the angels who trumpeted the birth of Christ. It always made Red grin to see the two men in their Roman–era garb with wings stuck to their backs, but she was grateful they didn't mind the roles. Their presence seemed to bring out some of the townsfolk who wouldn't normally attend.

She'd decided the event would be a perfect place to sell her baked goods and explain that the proceeds would be used to purchase the school supplies she needed. Already, the classroom was cold and drafty. She was sure the parents would want the children warm throughout the winter.

"Miss Meredith, do I have to say 'Hark, I see a bright light yonder'?" Jimmy Delaney asked, tugging at her arm. "Can't I just say, 'Hey, look at that light over there'?"

"That isn't how it's done, Jimmy," Reba Grainger scolded with her hand on her hip. She tossed her dark hair from her shoulder with her other hand. "Don't be a baby."

Red rolled her eyes. Perhaps she should have chosen Olive Mills for the roll of Mary, but Olive was inches shorter than Reba, and Trip was so much taller than both girls it would have looked awkward. She could have recast Joseph as well, she supposed, but Trip had actually requested the role and, in Red's opinion, deserved it.

"Reba, be polite," Red said. "Jimmy, the words stay just the way they are. If you don't want to say them, I can find another shepherd boy."

"Naw." Jimmy hung his head. "My ma would get mad and my pa would switch me."

She stifled a grin, knowing the boy was exaggerating. "Very well then. Take your place. Now does everyone have their lines written down?"

The children all nodded just as the door opened and Michael and Caroline walked in. Red continued on as if they hadn't arrived. "You're all positioned just like you'll stand on Christmas Eve. Practice your lines tonight and tomorrow we'll pick up from here. You can go now."

Like always, the children stampeded toward their coats and lunch boxes before they all filed out the door; all except for Trip, who seated himself at his desk and took out his extra work.

"Good afternoon," Red greeted Michael and Caroline.

"Good afternoon, Miss Red," Caroline replied. She bounced up and down in place, a bundle of excitement.

"Caroline," Red said, bending to her level. "In the classroom, you must call me Miss Meredith like the other children. All right?"

"All right."

"It wouldn't be right if you called me something else."

Caroline nodded.

"Let's get started," Red said then. She took Caroline's hand and led her to a vacant desk. She tried to forget Michael was watching her every move. "You can have a seat here every afternoon. For the next few days I'll test you on your current abilities. Then we'll work on some new things."

Walking to her own desk, Red went to open a drawer to retrieve a book for Caroline, only to have the drawer drop to the ground. "This blasted thing," she whispered. A new desk had been one of the items she'd requested from Elias Burton. The top of the one she used had been warped by a leak in the roof ages ago, the drawers were worn, and one leg was broken, making it wobbly.

"Here, let me help." She glanced up to see Michael standing beside her. "What's wrong with it?"

"Too much," she said with an edge of sarcasm and remembered how she'd compared his faults with the desk. "If you'd just help me lift the drawer back onto its track . . ."

Instead he knelt down and looked underneath the drawer. "You go on back to Caroline," he said. "I'll work on this. It'll keep me out of your way."

Red reluctantly walked away, keeping an eye on him as she went, watching him examine the desk. She supposed he had the skills to at least temporarily repair it. And she welcomed whatever he offered.

By the time she was through determining what Caroline's reading and writing skills were, Michael had stabilized the drawer and was smoothing his hand over the warped desk top with a critical eye.

"That should be enough for today," Red said to the girl. "You're very bright, Caroline. Your father has done a good job teaching you."

"Does that mean I can't come anymore?" Caroline's face crumbled.

"No, honey. You can come for as long as you like. I'm just pleased with how well you did."

Relieved, Caroline smiled.

"I fixed your drawer," Michael said then. "It's not going to last much longer, though."

"Well, it has to," Red told him matter–of–factly. "The school budget doesn't have the funds for a replacement." She looked around the simple room. "Or, according to Mr. Burton, another allotment of coal, new primers, catalogs, chalkboards, or chalk. We might be closing the doors once we run out."

Three pairs of eyes stared at her; Trip's were even wider than Caroline's and Michael's. Red waved her hand in a dismissive gesture. "Oh, don't listen to me. We'll get the supplies we need." She couldn't believe she'd spoken her concerns aloud. "But," she added to Michael, "A new desk is an unobtainable luxury." She shrugged. "I'll make do."

"Miss Meredith said I'm bright," Caroline chimed in.

"I already knew that," Michael replied. He placed his hand on her shoulder. "Guess we should let her get home, though. Thanks," he added to Red.

"My pleasure. I'll see you tomorrow, Caroline." She took a deep breath once they'd disappeared out the door.

The hour had gone well. Caroline was easy to work with, and Red hadn't made a fool of herself in front of Caroline's father. She hoped every day went as well.

Michael entered the barn that night and stared at the mounds of virgin wood and carpentry tools he'd brought with him from Philadelphia. They'd sat unused ever since.

A testament to his lost life, he touched one board linen, backed his hand away, then quickly snatched it up.

The baking began in earnest five days before the pageant. Signs of Christmas were all around, from the town square, which had wrappings of red ribbon around the lampposts, to Matthew and Tommy stringing berries for their hearths.

The scents of bread rising, pies and cakes baking, and the lingering snow from another early winter storm, buoyed Red's spirits and kept her mind from straying. She just knew her baking idea would be a success and was counting the days until she could make the selections from the coveted catalog she had and send the order on its way. If nothing else, she intended to prove to Elias Burton that she was resourceful and did not need his help. Perhaps that would earn her the respect she needed from the rest of the committee.

Preparations for the pageant were going smoothly as well. All the major players had studied their lines and stopped teasing each other. The one exception was the lack of an infant to play the Christ child. She hadn't realized that the youngest child in all of Ruley was two years old. And she couldn't see Ethan Mayers staying quietly in Reba's arms for long. He would want to run and play.

June and Kit and the other women in town who were expecting, weren't due to deliver until after the first of the year.

Standing in Kit's kitchen, the rest of the women in her family mixing or spooning or flouring, she lamented her predicament.

"I could try to get Caleb to sit still," April offered. "He's older than Ethan, so he might listen a bit better."

"I think your three–year–old, who is as big as a four–year–old, might be a bit too heavy for Reba," May teased.

"True. Caleb is rather large. Perhaps Reba, or rather, Mary, shouldn't hold the child this year."

"I have an idea," Caroline tried to interject. She was licking her fingers from the icing she and Sarah were applying to some cookies.

"Really, you'd think someone in this town would have an infant." June mixed a bowl of batter while contemplating. "Have you asked everyone if they have a sister or friend in Denver who has a baby?"

Red nodded. "Last week at church. Wanda's cousin has a six–month–old. A girl, but that doesn't matter. She would have been the perfect age, but the family left town last week to visit relatives back east."

"I have an idea," Caroline tried again.

"The whole world is expecting next month." Red finally looked to the child. "What idea, Caroline?"

"You can use Beth."

"Beth? Who's Beth?" Maddie asked.

"My baby doll," Caroline told her. "She has red hair like Miss Red, and Miss Red—I can call her that now 'cause we're not in school—helped me name her."

"A doll." April pondered the idea. "That just might work."

Red knelt down before Caroline. "Why, that's a wonderful idea, Caroline."

"Why didn't we think of that?" June added. "But does Beth have long hair? If so, you'd have to make it look short."

"We can do that." Red stood up and placed her hand on Caroline's shoulder. "You can bring Beth to class on Monday?"

Caroline beamed from her chair and nodded.

"Well then, I think you have solved our problem."

Later that afternoon, Red headed into town to check out the area where the pageant would come to life. The school committee and several parents had already set up a platform with hay strewn all around it. A wooden cradle sat empty in the middle and a large star hung from a pole overhead. On Wednesday night, the town would gather to sing songs and watch their children re-create the first Christmas. Then, after Trip's last line of, "And so a Child is born to us this day," there would be applause from the crowd, bows from the cast, and a short—she hoped—speech from the mayor, she'd announce her baked goods sale and petition for funds. She was sure everyone would respond. And they'd receive baked goods from the best bakers around.

Staring at the work the others had done, she realized her life had settled down. She was no longer worried about her pupils not wanting to learn—Trip had bounced back and had set the other struggling students on the same course, she was confident her idea to raise funds would work, and daily contact with Michael had lessened the anxiety she felt when he was around.

Not one for idleness, he'd taken to repairing everything from the squeak in the schoolroom door, to the loose shutters on the windows while she and Caroline worked. The first week alone he'd stabilized the leg on her desk, leveled the blackboard on the wall, and cleaned out the stove's smokestack. The room was warmer and less sooty for his efforts.

She'd thanked him many times over for his services, and he'd told her that he was just repaying her for tutoring Caroline. They'd managed to move on to a guarded friendship.

Though she still thought of him when she lay in bed at night, it was now with acceptance rather than animosity. And when she remembered the way he'd fingered her hair the day he'd asked her to teach Caroline, it was with a smile and a hitch in her breath. Her nerves tingled every time she relived the sensation; she'd learned to enjoy it.

"They call you Red," he'd said, as if he'd felt left out for not knowing. She'd assured him only her family was so familiar. That scene still caused her grief. The way he'd fingered her hair, told her about Caroline and her mother. He'd conveyed more to her that day than ever before. And she'd felt his pain. Again. She felt it always.

She knew if she had the power to bring back his wife and son, she would do so. She'd let them embrace one another and walk away together, their hearts mended again. She knew she would be able to put him from her mind then, once and for all, knowing he was happy.

But since she didn't have such power, and his wife and son were never coming back, she would sometimes dare to think that he was alone and she was alone, and Caroline needed a mother, and if only he could get over . . .

Then she'd come to her senses.

Like now. She looked beyond the town square, seeing Mr. Dortch sweeping the boardwalk outside his store, seeing Elias and Sheriff Moss talking outside the jail, and waving to Amelia as she unlocked the door to her restaurant.

Since she'd first seen the square, she'd always thought it would be nice to hold her wedding ceremony right where the pageant was held. She'd always felt the square was the center of everything that took place in Ruley. And Ruley had become a part of her. She enjoyed the tapestry of the small town and the people. She'd lived in New York all her life and had never thought she'd leave it until the opportunity came to visit her cousins. Everything had fallen into place after that; Kit needed a fresh start and there was a place for them in Ruley. Red didn't miss New York at all now.

Maybe one day she would marry. Maybe right there in the center of the square. She was beginning to doubt that more and more, but that didn't stop her from having dreams of being a wife and mother.

She didn't realize she'd traveled all the way home until she heard Maddie calling her name.

Her mind finally zeroed in on her friend.

"And what world were you just in?" Maddie replied.

Red exited the buggy and began to unharness her horse. "A make–believe world," she said.

She barely had time to put the finishing touches on the gifts she'd made for her family before it was time to leave for town. As always, the day before Christmas was busy. All day long she'd been frantically baking, sewing, and wrapping things for the pageant and her family. Now she and Maddie would travel to Kit's and Sam's for supper before they all headed to town.

This year, she and Maddie planned to spend the night at Kit's after the pageant. Tomorrow morning, after their gift exchange, they would join their cousins for Christmas dinner.

"Are you ready yet?" Maddie asked for the umpteenth time. She stood at the door, tapping her foot.

Red made one last glance around the room and mentally went over her mile–long list again. She had thread and needle for last minute costume mending, peppermint sticks for all the players, and family gifts for tomorrow morning. And she had a special gift for Caroline if, by chance, she and Michael came tonight. She hoped Michael would bring her so that Caroline could see Beth in her role.

"I hope so," she sighed, shaking away the image of Caroline and Michael alone tonight and on Christmas Day.

"If not, we'll make do," Maddie said and ushered her out the door. Ever the practical lady, nothing seemed to rattle Maddie's nerves. Not even, Red had noted, the impending arrival of her former beau. Smith Weatherby should arrive any day and yet, Madeline didn't appear to be fazed at all.

Why, then, did everyone know when Red was "aflutter," as her sister had put it? It certainly wasn't fair.

The evening passed by in a whirl. The town square sparkled with bright lights, the crowd was large and noisy, the players better than Red expected, and her bake sale a success.

Local miners down from the Rockies to stock up on

winter supplies purchased the largest portion of the goods, treats they hadn't had in many a day, and they all commented on how wonderful they tasted.

Only one incident threatened to spoil Red's evening, and that was when Elias approached her after she'd made her announcement. Taking her arm, he'd attempted to steer her away from the table where a line had already formed, whispering, "What do you think you're doing?"

She'd pulled her arm free, furious that he thought he could grab her so. Kit and Maddie, who had been taking customer orders, surrounded her for added support. "What don't you understand, Mr. Burton?" she'd replied. "You stated on several occasions that there were no funds for our much needed supplies, so I decided to raise my own. Is there something wrong with that?"

Elias eyed Maddie and Kit and quickly regained his temper. "You should have informed me. Received permission first."

"The thought didn't even enter my mind," Red told him. A moment later, the other two school committee members arrived. April, May, and June shielded the customers from view and kept selling the baked goods while Fred Barlow said, "I think we need to talk, Elias."

"Now's a good time," Lavyrle Hancock added.

They'd left her before she knew it, and Red hadn't had time to worry about the outcome of their discussion. She focused on her customers instead.

They were still counting the funds when Caroline ran up to her and hugged her skirts. Red saw Michael not far behind his daughter. He smiled and Red felt her heart quicken.

"Miss Red, Miss Red, this is the bestest night," Caroline cried.

"Did you like the pageant?" Red knelt down to talk to Caroline.

"Oh, it was so beautiful," Caroline replied. "And Beth did such a good job as the baby Jesus."

"Yes, she did. And because you were kind enough to share her, I have a small gift for you." She took the brown wrapped box from her pocket, looked to Michael for his approval, and then gave it to Caroline.

"A gift, for me?" Caroline sucked in her breath.

"Now when we braid your hair we'll have something to bind it with."

"A ribbon! A pink one! My very own pink ribbon! Oh thank you, Miss Red! Thank you, thank you!" Caroline wrapped her arms around Red's neck.

Red returned the embrace, drawing from Caroline's warmth, relishing in the feel of the child in her arms. She knew she'd come to love Caroline as if she were her own. "I'm glad you like it, Caroline," she whispered. "Happy Christmas, honey."

"This is the bestest gift," Caroline claimed before glancing up at her father. "Except for the gifts you give me, Papa."

"No need to worry about hurting my feelings, Buttercup. Miss Red's gift is the bestest," he added with a wink.

Red fought back a swelling of emotion.

"But, but I don't have a gift for you," the child protested. She cupped Red's cheek with her chubby, mitten-encased hand.

"I don't need a gift, sweetheart. Just seeing you happy is the only gift I need."

"Oh, I am happy tonight," Caroline said. "I have you and Sarah and Papa. And soon we'll all go skating. That will make me more happy. Papa, can I take off my mittens and feel how smooth my ribbon is?"

"Just don't lose them."

Red helped Caroline remove her gloves and stuffed them in her pocket. Then she stood up. "I hope you don't mind my giving her a present," she said to Michael.

"Guess I figured you would. You're that way," he replied.

"I am?" She burrowed deeper into her coat, not sure if his words were a compliment or a criticism.

When the sides of his mouth lifted slightly, making Red draw in a breath, making her feel more vulnerable, she concluded they were a compliment. "You are," he whispered.

"Can I go show Sarah my ribbon?" Caroline interrupted them. "Can I, Papa, please?"

Michael scanned the area and pointed to Sarah who was standing on the stage platform. "She's right over there. You can tell her goodnight and get Beth while you're at it."

Caroline fled like a bullet, leaving Red and Michael alone under the sparkling lights. The crowd had thinned, but several people were still milling around. Someone laughed and others joined him. A girl called out for her brother to stop teasing her, and a woman called her daughter to her side.

As far as Red was concerned, the night had grown quiet. "Well," she finally said. "I guess I'd better start cleaning up. I don't know why we wait until Christmas Eve to put on this pageant. It leaves everyone exhausted for Christmas Day.

"Next year I'm definitely going to move it up a week. I said that last year too but never followed through." She laughed softly, more from nerves than her rambling words. "You'd think I'd learn."

Michael smiled with her. "If you'd like, I'll help you, Meredith," he replied.

Her laughter lodged in her throat. He'd never called her by her real name before. The sound of it on his lips, though strange, was also fulfilling.

"It's the least I can do," he added, smiling again.

Red managed to nod in reply and moved toward the tables that needed their attention.

Chapter Six

When the rooster crowed hours later, Michael had just finished covering the object he'd loaded into his wagon. He stood back, rubbed his tired eyes, and concluded he was satisfied. After leaving town last night, he'd taken Caroline home, tucked her into bed, and headed for the barn. He'd been up all night finishing the project he'd started weeks before.

He was pleased with his work. Pleased his skills were as sharp as they had been years ago, pleased he'd been able to battle his inner demons and complete the job.

Now he just needed to give the project away. No simple task. Not only was he punchy from lack of sleep, but self–consciousness had grabbed hold and wasn't letting go. He wasn't quite sure he had it in him to face Meredith and give her the gift.

Rubbing his hand over his face he thought about putting the wagon in the barn and skipping out altogether on joining her family for Christmas dinner. From last night's conversation with her, he was sure she didn't even know he and Caroline had been invited.

He'd accepted Travis's invitation several days ago because, at the time, the alternative—spending the day alone with Caroline—had appealed to him even less. And he'd thought it would be the perfect opportunity to give Meredith her gift.

He was still surprised the family hadn't strung him up by his thumbs after his insensitive remark, but he was grateful they hadn't. He and Caroline had come to rely on their company. Being with them helped pass time, provided Caroline with the friendship she needed, and—since he was being more honest with himself these days after taking some of Pastor Johnson's messages to heart—he had to admit they had provided him with the fellowship he needed as well.

He'd shut himself off from the world after Claire and Daniel died. He'd done so deliberately, knowing full well what he was doing. It was difficult to break out of that comfortable place he'd retreated to, hard not to fall back into something that fit so well. For his daughter's sake and his own he was trying to emerge from the cloak he'd wrapped them in.

He had Meredith to thank—or blame, depending on how he viewed things from one minute to the next. Her insistence that Caroline needed friends and her refusal to back down or be bullied by him had made all the difference.

He still wasn't sure how he felt about the changes, but he knew he felt lighter, as if the anchor he'd weighed himself down with wasn't as heavy. If he thought too long and too hard about the past few weeks, though, he began to panic. Like now with the prospect of his motives being scrutinized. He wasn't even sure what his motives were.

Maybe he'd be better off waiting until he could present Meredith with the gift when they were alone or after he'd had a good night's sleep. He had a little girl who would be excited when she woke; she would demand most of the energy he had left. Before he'd headed to the barn last night, he'd made sure there was a stocking hanging on the mantel with some special treats inside, and he'd tied the doll cradle he'd made with a red bow he'd impulsively bought at the mercantile last week. The past two years he'd barely been able to wish his daughter a merry Christmas, and there had been no gifts.

This year he'd felt different. Better. He still missed his son. Always would. And his wife, the way she'd sparkled long ago. He'd always wish they hadn't died, but he couldn't change reality. For Caroline's sake, he knew it was time to move on. It would help if he knew where they were headed. Managing to spend Christmas Day with Meredith and her family was a start if he could muster the mettle.

He rubbed his eyes again, knowing he had to try. Then he made his way to the house, aware that his precious daughter would be up and about in a very short while.

Red sank into the cushioned chair inside May's parlor and closed her eyes. The children were playing with their new toys in the Worths' front yard, and Kit, May, June, April, and Maddie were setting the dining table for turkey dinner, and Sam, Travis, Will, and Luke were outside smoking the cigars Sam had received earlier in the day. Red decided it was time to excuse herself from all the activity and take a much–needed break.

She was still exhausted from last night's activities and rising early this morning hadn't helped. But she would have never allowed herself to miss a moment of Christmas Day for something as silly as sleep. She could still feel the warmth of Maddie and Kit's hands holding hers as Sam led them in a prayer of thanks before they'd devoured the griddlecakes he'd made. And she could still hear the laughter reverberating through Kit's home as they exchanged simple gifts of affection. When they'd arrived at May's, where the rest of the family had already gathered, the noise level had shot up as the children spotted all their new gifts.

Only one thing threatened Red's joy, and that was knowing that Caroline and Michael were alone. She soothed herself by remembering how Caroline's eyes had widened and her mouth had formed an O at the

sight of the pink ribbon Red had given her and how the
child had hugged her and thanked her for the gift, but
Red found herself longing to see her again and fretting.

And then she realized her futile thoughts were the
reason she rarely paused to rest. Every time she did,
they became relentless. She could only imagine how
hard it was for them on days like today. She knew only
too well the loneliness they must feel. She was blessed
to be surrounded by her extended family, true, but it
wasn't the same as having a spouse and children.

She got to her feet, opening her eyes at the same
time, deciding she had to redirect her thoughts. She
took a step and halted. "Michael . . . er, Mr. Wisdom."
Her heart somersaulted.

"Happy Christmas," he said quietly, his hat in his
hands. His cheeks were a bit flushed from the chill of
the day. His eyes were red, as if he'd been up all night.
He wore his nice overcoat, ironed dungarees, and polished boots. The white of his shirt enhanced his
sun–bronzed face. "Guess I startled you."

"Startled" didn't begin to describe how Red felt. She
tugged on the sleeves of her royal blue bodice as the
lace grew tight around her throat. "I didn't know you
were here. Caroline too? I was just resting."

"So I saw," he told her. He had too. It hadn't lasted
long, but she'd been seated in the chair with her eyes
closed and her face relaxed and softened. She'd looked
prettier than that morning's sunrise, her burnished hair

loose about her face and shoulders, no pins or hat to hide it away. "I didn't mean to disturb you."

"No. You didn't." She took a deep breath and exhaled. "And Happy Christmas to you too."

"You didn't know we were coming, did you?"

"No. You should have told me last night. I'd have saved Caroline's gift."

"Are you kidding? She was so excited to have something new to wear today. It looks pretty in her hair."

Red shyly covered her smile with her hand and glanced at his big, weathered hands. "Getting it to stay must have been difficult for you."

"I'll be relieved when she can do it herself." He motioned his shoulder toward the window. "She's outside. She's waiting for us."

"Us?"

"We, that is, Caroline and I, have a gift for you," he told her. "Outside."

He saw her eyes widen, then the beginnings of another smile before it faded away. "I . . . I can't accept . . . I don't want . . . expect . . ."

"Come see before you decide." He moved forward. Her eyes widened as he reached for her hand. The moment of connection shook his entire frame. Her hand fit comfortably into his own just like she had when she'd fallen into his arms. It was warm, soft, and smooth. Something he hadn't felt in such a long time.

Surely he'd already made a fool of himself, surely he

was going to continue to, so he fought away the strong emotions threatening him and led her outside.

Red struggled with the same emotions. Her head was spinning, her heart was thumping, and her skin was tingling. She'd just been sitting in the chair daydreaming about him. Feeling sorry for herself, and him, and then he was there. She hadn't had time to assimilate the suddenness of it all before his strong hand had caught her own. She only knew that she never wanted him to let go.

Please Lord, don't ever let him let go, she silently prayed, knowing how foolish the request was.

She let him steer her outside. She saw her sister and cousins and Maddie had joined the men and children in front of Michael's wagon. What in the world was going on?

Caroline was there as well and inside the bed was a large item covered with linens.

"Miss Red! Miss Red!" Caroline bounced up and down near the wagon. "Happy Christmas, Miss Red. Papa and me brought you a present."

"Happy Christmas, Caroline," Red replied absently. "Really, Mr. Wisdom, this isn't necessary or . . ."

"Quiet," he told her. "I'll give a gift to anyone I please. That anyone happens to be you at the moment."

She looked at him with shock on her face but held her tongue. Then he was releasing her hand.

"Stay right here," he said and planted her alongside the wagon. He then climbed into the bed. "I decided that desk of yours had to go. And since I knew there wasn't any money to replace it," he snapped the sheet aside, "I made you a new one."

Red's mouth dropped open as everyone else gasped. Inside the wagon was the most beautiful desk she had ever seen. "You . . . you . . . you . . . *made* this? For *me*?" Was it possible?

"Do you like it? Papa worked real hard," Caroline said. The child wrapped her arms around Red's legs. "He stayed up all night to finish it."

Red pressed her hand to her mouth even as she hugged Caroline close and stared at her father. No one had ever given her such a gift. She wasn't sure what to do.

"Oh, Red," Kit whispered. "It's lovely. I can't imagine the effort Mr. Wisdom put into such a beautiful piece of furniture."

"Come on up here," Michael said and extended his hand to help her up. Caroline giggled, but it took Red a moment to move. When she did, the thought crossed her mind that she was going to be able to touch him again.

Then he was lifting her into the wagon. "Go ahead, look it over," Michael offered.

She ran her hand over the wood's smooth grain, marveling at the richness and texture. There were three drawers on each side and a long narrow drawer in the middle, all opened effortlessly.

"Oh, my," she finally managed. "I can't believe this."

"I hope you like it," he said.

"I . . ." She looked at him again and felt tears, hot and swift, fill her eyes. Fat drops slid out before she could wipe them away. She didn't even bother. "You must know how incredible this is. I don't know what to say. You . . . you . . . I love it. I just can't believe . . . Why?"

Her emerald eyes glistened. The sun caught her hair and transformed it from vibrant brown to shimmering burgundy and every shade in–between. She had the palest, smoothest skin he'd ever seen, marred only by the enticing few freckles dotting her nose.

How he itched to run the back of his hand down her smooth cheek, to cup the back of her head and draw her close until their lips touched and she melted against him.

"You needed a desk," he said instead, matter–of–fact-ly. His answer was the furthest thing from the truth, but to tell her otherwise would have been too costly. "I can bring it by the schoolhouse tomorrow afternoon if you want me to. I know it's Saturday and all, but then you'll have it in place for school on Monday morning. Can you make the time to meet me there?"

"Time?" Red shook her head to clear it. "Of course I'll make the time. Just tell me when. Oh, Michael, this is incredible. I'm still stunned."

"You do fine workmanship, Michael," Travis inter-rupted them. "I've been wanting a new desk of my own. Maybe we need to talk."

"Papa made my baby doll a bed," Caroline added. "It rocks back and forth."

"A cradle?" Red looked from Caroline to Michael for his answer.

He shrugged. "The doll had to have a place to sleep." He jumped from the wagon, wrapped his hands around Red's waist and effortlessly lifted her down in front of him. "Let's discuss what you're looking for, Travis," he added, even as he held her gaze and smiled. Far from shadowed, his eyes were full of satisfaction and something Red never thought she'd recognize: promise.

Then Sam was handing him a cigar and the children were scattering. May announced that dinner would be ready in just a few minutes.

Red stayed where she was, still in shock, amazement, and filled with joy all the way to her toes, because not only had she just received a wonderful gift; she'd also received a hint of something more, and for the first time in her life she knew she was in love.

Chapter Seven

She arrived at the schoolhouse just after noon on Saturday after a solid night's sleep; only sheer exhaustion had made it possible. But the moment her eyes had snapped opened at dawn, she'd scrambled out of bed.

Michael had built her a desk, crafted it with his own hands, and was bringing it to the school for her. She was thrilled beyond imagination and still found yesterday's event hard to believe.

She helped Maddie with their multitude of chores throughout the morning, stored the pageant materials away in the attic for another year, and finally killed enough time so she could head for town.

She was nearly bursting with excitement; she couldn't wait to see Michael and confirm that it hadn't all been a dream. She couldn't wait to sit behind her new desk, stock it with supplies, and thank Michael a hundred more times.

Once again she marveled at how just last month she'd fretted over her teaching abilities, her pupils' lack of interest, the ignorance of some of the men—Michael included—and the dire situation of the school budget. And how, now, everything had turned around. Her students were excited again, especially Trip, the pageant had been successful, the bake sale as well, and she had a new desk.

Last night's Christmas dinner, with Michael and Caroline and the rest of her family around her, had been wonderful.

She'd even come to the conclusion that she loved Michael. The uncertainty of a future with him was small discomfort considering the rest. She had no illusions about his love for his wife, his pain about the past. If unrequited love was her future she would accept it.

Seeing him on occasion would dull the ache. Tutoring Caroline had given her the opportunity to get to know him better, given them the opportunity to become, if not friends, at least friendly. She understood now that his gruffness was born out of his intense pain. That losing his wife and son had reshaped him. Never having experienced anything so tragic in her own life, she was in no position to judge the constraints he'd placed on Caroline's activities or the constraints he'd placed on himself. She might have reacted the very same way had she lost a son and husband.

The anger and frustration she had felt toward him only a month ago had evolved into compassion. And now she felt as if she was getting glimpses of the other Michael, the Michael that had called to her ever since the moment they'd met last July.

She admitted to herself now that she had been attracted to him from the very beginning. The day Trip fell from the tree had sealed it. Kit had noticed the following Sunday. All the women in her family had noticed. Red had denied it. She denied it no longer.

At least to herself. She would keep her love for Michael her own private secret. A prized possession she would cherish. She wouldn't dwell on thoughts of a long, lonely future, of the husband and children of her own she'd never have. Instead she'd look forward to afternoons when Michael and Caroline walked into her classroom. Caroline would run ahead of her father and hug Red's skirts, and Michael would grin slightly, remove his hat, and smooth his wavy brown hair.

That would be enough.

It would have to be.

Today, Red would receive an added treat; he was bringing her a desk made by his own hands. Her frame tingled just thinking about it.

When she heard the door creak open, she stopped removing books from a drawer in her old desk and smiling, glanced up.

Her smile immediately fell away when she saw Elias Burton in the doorway instead of Michael.

"Mr. Burton," she said, struggling to recover. "What brings you here on a Saturday?"

Elias shut the door behind him. "What brings me here?" He was a tall man, tall and thin. Most called him handsome, but Red had never been able to convince herself so. Now, her feelings for Michael clear, she understood why.

"I believe I asked that question, yes." She rose, clasped her hands in schoolmarm fashion and planted her feet for what she assumed was going to be a confrontation. "What can I help you with?"

"You shouldn't have done what you did, Meredith," he said, advancing into the room slowly.

"I'm guessing you're talking about the bake sale since you made your opinion quite clear at the pageant."

"You'd be guessing right."

"I don't understand what has you so upset, Mr. Burton. I raised money to support this school. *After* you told me there would be no funds forthcoming. What is so wrong with that?"

"What's wrong with that is it gave others the impression I wasn't doing my job." He stopped beside her desk and fingered the stack of books on its top.

"Well, perhaps you and the rest of the committee aren't doing your job," she replied stiffly.

"Oh, I'm doing my job all right." His upper lip curled. "After I explained to Hancock and Barlow that the budget was short so I could give them a bonus, they backed off. In fact, they approved my new year's agenda, and the first piece of business is to inform you that your services are no longer needed. We're dismissing you."

"You're . . . what?" Red's knees nearly buckled.

"Just because you didn't get everything on your wish list for unnecessary trinkets—"

"Coal is unnecessary? Readers? Chalk?"

"—didn't give you the right to stir up the town with your dire predictions that their children would suffer."

"It's true," she stated.

"And the pageant was not the place to make your solicitation."

"Solicitation?"

"You demonstrated poor judgment and therefore the committee has decided to dismiss you."

Red was too stunned to speak.

"By the looks of things—" He fingered the books again. "It appears you were cleaning out your desk. How coincidental."

He eyed her for a long while before he turned and strode back to the door. "It could have been very different, Meredith," he said. "An alliance between us would have profited us both greatly. I pictured you on my arm for years to come. And your family helping us become very powerful." He paused, his hand on the doorknob. "I'll return this afternoon to make sure you've removed all your personal items. Leave the key to the door on your desk."

"Who–who–who is going to be here Monday to greet the children?"

"That's no longer your concern," he replied and closed the door behind him.

Red stared at the door as her body began to shake. She'd been dismissed? Just like that? She was no longer the school's teacher?

It wasn't possible. The schoolhouse was *hers*. The children were *hers*.

Teaching was her *life*.

Dear God. *Oh, dear God!* What had just happened?

She buried her head in her hands, rehearing Elias's words. He'd said she'd demonstrated poor judgment. Stirred the town up. All because of a bake sale? She'd been dismissed because of a bake sale?

This couldn't be happening. He'd return shortly and tell her he was lying. Tell her he'd just wanted to frighten her.

When the door did open she felt her heart surge with hope. But this time Michael was the man who stood inside the frame.

Oh, God! she silently screamed again, and burst into tears.

Her reaction wasn't what he'd been expecting. He'd thought about it all night. Considering her excitement yesterday, he'd decided she just might kiss his cheek, or at least embrace him. She'd be smiling for certain. She might even drop her lashes in embarrassment since she wouldn't be able to contain her excitement.

He'd left Caroline at Sarah's just in case the kiss came about. Lucky for him, the Caulder ranch was within walking distance from his place and on the way to town.

All the way here he'd thought about what his reaction would be. What he'd want it to be. He'd decided he just might kiss Meredith back. Or hug her back. Or drop his own gaze, not in embarrassment, but just so he wouldn't be tempted to draw her to him, embarrass himself in a different way.

He certainly hadn't expected tears. Sad tears at that. Had she changed her mind about the desk? Had she decided she disliked him too much to accept it?

He felt the hair on his neck begin to rise, felt his face heat. A couple of weeks ago his anger would have had its own way and he'd have probably walked out, but words the pastor had just read last Sunday rushed through his brain. *Do not be eager in your heart to be angry, For anger resides in the bosom of fools,* he'd quoted. So Michael took a steadying breath and moved into the room. He wasn't going to assume he was the cause of her tears. He wasn't going to assume anything.

"Meredith?" he said to her bent figure, seated in her chair, her head in her hands.

She looked up, wet tracks marring her cheeks. "I'm sorry," she said and sniffed. "I never cry." She smacked her hands across her face. "Your arrival was just too much."

"My arrival?" The heat rose again. He held it at bay.

She sniffed again, stood, squared her shoulders, and said, "Yes. So soon after Elias Burton's departure. He just informed me that I no longer have a position with the town. I am no longer the teacher." The last words she said on a sob.

"He did what?" Michael's temper began to build for a different reason. Meredith wasn't upset with him. But she'd been dismissed?

"It appears he and the members of the committee took exception to my having a bake sale to raise money for the school." Droplets of tears still clung to her long lashes. She rubbed her brow. "I'm told I didn't use proper judgment. Therefore, I've been . . . been terminated."

Michael flexed his hands but held them at his sides as her control nearly slipped and her bottom lip quivered.

"I'm sure my replacement will appreciate the new desk, Mr. Wisdom."

"Like hell," he grumbled.

"Excuse me?"

He flexed his hands again, but lost the battle to keep them still. He took Meredith's arms instead, his thumbs skimming over the pale yellow worsted wool she wore. "That no–account fired you? Because you held a bake sale?"

"Those were his words."

"What he meant was, he fired you because you solved a problem he couldn't. Which made him look like the fool he is."

"I agree with you, but it doesn't matter why, although I appreciate your viewpoint. The bottom line is that I no longer work here."

"If you think I'm leaving *your* desk for someone else, think again."

"But, Mic–Mr. Wisdom," she argued. "I can't take it home with me. It belongs here."

"And so do you. My daughter needs you. So does Trip and the rest of these kids."

She blinked away fresh tears. "How can he do this?"

"He can't. He won't. We'll see about this."

"What are you going to do?"

"For starters?" Michael asked. "This." He kissed her. Just like he'd decided he'd do. Except he didn't wait for her to kiss him first. And it wasn't on the cheek.

But he hadn't reckoned that kissing her would make his heart slam against his chest. It nearly beat right out of his skin. He hadn't counted on the fresh autumn scent of her spiraling around him, drawing him like a bee to honey.

He pulled her closer, realized she was kissing him back, and Michael did what he'd craved from the moment he'd seen her sitting in her buggy all prim and proper in front of his house months ago; he slid his hand into her silky hair and let his fingers dance through the flaming tresses.

It was as mind–boggling as he'd thought it would be. His head swirled from the headiness. Meredith's warm mouth, her incredible hair, her sorrow. He heard her ragged mew, felt her hands cautiously touch his shoulders, and then her nails dig into his skin.

Was there anything more right than this moment?

With reluctance he broke the kiss, stood toe–to–toe with her and gazed into her vivid green eyes.

She wasn't going to be hurt like this. Not when he could do something about it. And this time he could do something.

"What are you going to do?" she asked again, her voice low and raspy.

"I'm going to find out just what Elias Burton thinks he's doing," he told her and strode to the door.

Chapter Eight

She trailed him moments later, knowing that regardless of the outcome with Elias, she wouldn't have changed anything leading up to her dismissal. Not when it had inspired Michael to kiss her.

She was still trying to catch her breath. She could still feel Michael's strong hands taking her arms, his dark eyes sparkling with indignation. And something else.

Desire?

Everything was still replaying in her mind. The touch of him. The taste of him. The masculine scent of wood and wind and sweat and soap. And now he was going to stand up for her. It was too much to take in all at once.

She was sure Elias had met his match. She recognized too, that Michael *needed* to do what he was doing. Perhaps because he'd been unable to save his

wife and son? Knowing so caused her to consider that
his kiss might have been spawned by his need to rescue
her and nothing more. Merely a reaction born of his
past. Just in case, she wasn't going to place her hopes
in other possibilities. But she would cherish the most
incredible moment of her life and live it over again and
again, the feel of his lips on hers, the giddiness of it all.
Her knees were still weak. Her breath still hitched. And
her heart had never soared so high.

Elias Burton had done her a favor and he didn't even
know it. For that alone she'd suffer the outcome. But she
couldn't sit calmly by while Michael confronted him.

She hurried outside, thinking he would just be
pulling away from the school in his wagon. Instead she
found he'd unhitched his horse, left the wagon
behind—her desk still inside it—and was already gone.

As a cold wind whipped around her and a trail of billowing white clouds began to stain the vivid blue sky,
she searched the road for any sign of him. Seeing no
one she returned inside, grabbed her coat from a peg on
the wall, and made her way to her buggy. It would
begin snowing soon, she determined. Hopefully not
until she had caught up with him.

Michael didn't know Elias Burton or where he might
find him, but he was certain Mr. Dortch, the owner of
the local mercantile, would. Dortch bragged that he
knew anyone and everyone this side of Denver. He'd
lived in the territory longer than anyone so Michael had

no reason to doubt him, even if he hesitated asking the man, knowing it would be all over town within minutes. Short of returning to ask Meredith where Burton lived, or one of her kin, there wasn't much else to be done.

"On Third Street, next to Dr. Worth's place," Dortch told him with planted hands on the counter in his store and a raised brow. "Burton's going places, you know. He'll put Ruley on the map one day. Going to run for mayor next year. Wouldn't doubt if he became governor one day."

"He's politically inclined, is he?" Michael asked. He calmly withdrew a licorice stick from a jar and tossed Dortch a coin to pay for it.

"I was going to run for mayor myself till Burton made his intentions clear. He's got that, that, what do you call it, charisma about him. Made me change my mind."

"Did he now?" A lot of politicians were good at fooling people. It seemed Burton had most of the town fooled. But not Meredith Wilde. And she'd gotten in his way.

"Not that all of us cotton to him or his granddaddy before he died," Mrs. Dortch added. She dusted the jar lid Michael had just opened, then leaned forward conspiratorially. "Came out here after some scandal in the family. Acted as if they were our betters, they did. Humph. The younger would have you believe he's pert' near perfect. Well I'll tell you, I don't trust the man."

Michael hid his grin. But he enjoyed hearing Mrs. Dortch's opinion.

"Now, Mother," Mr. Dortch chided. "Don't go stirring things." He looked to Michael. "You got business with Burton? Decided to put your girl in school?"

"Something like that," Michael said. He tipped his hat and tucked the licorice into his pocket, then made his way outside. The temperature had dipped in the few minutes since he stepped into the store, forcing him to pull up his coat collar when the wind bit into his neck.

He mounted his horse and rode toward the stately houses on Third Street, his temper in check but his resolve firm. Burton would reinstate Meredith before the day was out or suffer the consequences. So he wanted to be a politician, huh? Michael would see just how much.

He knocked on Burton's door and waited. A maid answered a few moments later and saw him to the parlor. Burton descended the stairs soon after, and Michael stood when he entered.

"Mr. Wisdom?" Burton said, "I don't believe we've met." He moved to shake Michael's hand, but Michael sat back down instead.

"You'd be right, Mr. Burton," he replied. "Never would have either, except I happened to be delivering something to the schoolhouse today."

The man's eyes widened.

"I heard what you did."

"A mutually agreed upon decision," Burton replied. "What makes that your concern?"

"My daughter makes it my concern. What makes you think it was mutually agreed upon? I spoke with Miss Wilde soon after you left. I came away with a different impression."

Burton eyed Michael before he strode to a cherry-wood table and poured a snifter of brandy. He sipped the liquid himself instead of offering it to Michael. He was formally dressed for supper in a black suit and cravat. By the elegant looks of the house, everything in Burton's life was orderly and sophisticated.

He was sure Burton thought the elaborate surroundings and his haughty attitude would rattle Michael; that if he waited long enough, Michael would get anxious and leave. He was wrong. Michael had been married to the daughter of the wealthiest man in Philadelphia. If Harold Grainger hadn't been able to rattle him—and he'd tried—Burton surely wouldn't succeed.

"What's your interest, Mr. Wisdom?" he asked after several silent moments. "More so, what were you delivering at the schoolhouse?"

"I'll be frank with you, Burton," Michael told him. He left the sofa, strode toward the window, and then spun to face the man. "I came here to tell you that whatever you're up to is going to backfire. While you and me and Miss Wilde are the only people who know what you've done, you still have the time to reverse it. Once word leaks, it'll be too late. Have you thought this through? Do you know what the good citizens of Ruley are going to do once they hear their beloved teacher is gone? And believe me, she *is* their beloved teacher. Do you know what the children will do? They adore her. My daughter adores her, and I've seen it with the other kids.

"I'd be guessing about what your motive is here. Sure, she showed the town that you're not on top of your job."

"Now see here."

"But you went for the jugular and that was a bit rough in my opinion. A firm chastisement maybe, no salary increase next year. Those things would have been in order. Maybe.

"But it seems to me something else motivated you to dismiss her. She's a pretty woman, Burton. I'm sure you've noticed. Did you find yourself enamored by her? Did she rebuff your overtures?"

Burton snickered. "I'm not attracted to Meredith Wilde in the least." He slammed the snifter down on a table. "She exercised poor judgment. She doesn't take no for an answer. Soliciting the good people of Ruley to buy her second–rate baked goods was outrageous. And it backfired on her."

Michael pondered his response, then said, "Think again, Burton. The way I see it, you're embarrassed because she found a way to make money when you and your committee members couldn't. Or didn't even try. To be fair, I'll be asking them for their own opinion of what went down. I'm pretty sure most everyone will see the truth when I get through explaining how worried she was about their children taking a chill and not learning to their full potential. And, when I'm through, they'll be wanting to take your job from you instead of the other way around."

"Now see here," Burton exploded. "I don't know who you think you are or why I should listen to this cockamamie story of yours but—"

"I'm a parent," Michael shouted back. "A parent who has a real concern for the way you're running things." He lowered his voice when he knew he had Burton's attention. "Now like I said, while this is still between the three of us you have time to reverse it. Word will reach the Caulders, the Worths, the Harts, and the Honors in no time at all. Do you think these fine upstanding people of the community will allow you to dismiss not only their children's teacher, but their cousin and sister as well? I think you'd better give their influence a bit more thought."

Burton's face went from red to white.

"I guess you didn't think this through."

The door chime caused both men to hush. The maid entered with Meredith behind her.

"Mr. Wisdom," she said. "Mr. Burton." She was paler than normal, her freckles more prominent. Tension radiated from her. Michael wanted to close the space between them, tell her everything was going to be all right but he remained where he was instead.

"Miss Wilde," he replied.

"Well, well," Burton drawled. "As if one unwanted

guest weren't enough. Join us, Meredith. Your friend here has been pleading your cause and attempting to persuade me to change my mind."

"And I appreciate his effort, Mr. Burton." She stepped further into the room, her chin high. She clasped her shaking hands and bit her quivering bottom lip. "He'll never know how much. But Mr. Wisdom is a busy man. He doesn't have time to spend on this kind of nonsense. Neither do I."

"Then both of you may leave at any time."

"Mr. Wisdom," Red went on. "I'm more than capable of handling this myself. Please don't trouble yourself any longer on my account. I'm sure Caroline is waiting for you."

"I'll worry about Caroline if it's all the same to you," Michael told her. "And I'll leave after you've been reinstated," he added.

She smiled slightly and he saw her shoulders relax. "Very well. Thank you." She turned to Burton. "Elias, I've thought about this all the way here. I realize you were embarrassed by the baked goods sale. And rightly so. But not because of what I did. You were embarrassed because you did nothing to assist and everyone knew it.

"You're attempting to use me as a scapegoat and I won't allow it. I've done nothing to warrant dismissal."

"Miss Wilde, I'm doing nothing of the—"

"I'm not finished," Red interrupted. "You insinuated that I could have prevented all of this if I had only looked favorably upon your attempts to court me," she went on. "That you had envisioned a strong alliance between us."

"Is that so?" Michael asked. He eyed Burton and watched him shuffle his feet.

"I'm convinced you are upset because I refused you. And I'm more convinced than ever that I refused you because I knew you were a devious, immoral person whom I didn't want to associate with. I'll tell everyone exactly how many times you requested I dine with you if you don't recant my dismissal. And just so you're aware, I plan to make it known that the school funds were improperly used for bonuses."

"Weren't we just discussing this, Burton?" Michael added. "Spurned after all, were you?"

"Don't be ridiculous." Burton poured himself another brandy, swirling it in his snifter while crossing his feet and leaning against the hearth's mantel. "You must be delusional, Miss Wilde. I've never approached you for a more personal relationship."

"Be careful, Elias," Red told him. "Trip Dawson heard everything you said on your last visit."

The man choked on the brandy he sipped.

Michael grinned. "I suppose Miss Wilde and I will have to take this news to the rest of the town since you're not willing to cooperate."

"I'd prefer no one be told anything," Meredith concurred. "If you would just reinstate me, we could forget this entire episode."

"Or perhaps you're willing to risk your budding political career and the wrath of Ruley's good citizens?"

Burton set down his snifter and sank into a black velvet wing chair, crossing his legs and moving one foot like a pendulum back and forth. Michael could almost see him calculating his position. It was obvious Burton would have to back down, but men like him would try anything, wait until all possible leverage had been played before giving in.

He finally shrugged. "Perhaps I was a bit hasty, Meredith," he said, getting to his feet. "I was very disturbed by your childish behavior. I can see now that I allowed my anger to get the best of me."

"And what childish behavior would that be?" Meredith countered. She took a step toward Burton. Michael could tell the anger she'd held in check was about to explode. "I'll reiterate, Mr. Burton. I did nothing wrong. You have no cause to dismiss me. No cause for anger. And if my reputation is impaired by you in any way I will shout the truth to anyone I can and dog your every step. I might even become a candidate for mayor and run against you."

Burton laughed until he saw Red meant every word. "Women are fighting for the right to vote, Mr. Burton. Don't discount us."

She took a breath, and Michael grinned again. He'd been a recipient of her tongue lashing a time or two, but he wondered if she realized the power she held.

"I believe Mr. Burton understands now, Miss Wilde, that his decision was wrong," he said in the quiet that followed. "And I'm sure in the future he'll use more restraint when making decisions that affect the entire town." He took a step closer to her, could smell the clean flowery scent of her that made him recall their kiss. The kiss he'd tried not to think about since leaving the schoolhouse. He'd tried to focus on confronting Burton instead, because Meredith Wilde was a good teacher and the children needed her and because Caroline needed her and because Burton had done an injustice that needed correcting.

There were other reasons. He couldn't deny them any longer, but now was not the time to summon them to mind. He'd wait until he was alone and the walls weren't closing in on him. Then the memory of her scent could overtake him. And he'd allow it.

At present he took her arm to steady them both. "Well, Burton," he said in a even, relaxed drawl, "Ruley's school teacher and I are going to be leaving now. We're going to return to the schoolhouse and unload the new desk I made for her. And she's going to put her books and supplies inside. Maybe a personal token on top. Come Monday she'll be there when the children arrive. And you are going to let the good people of Ruley know what a fine teacher she is."

"As you said, Mr. Wisdom, the children need Miss Wilde. Who am I to stand in the way of educating them?"

Meredith smirked. "Indeed."

"There is one other thing," Michael went on in a firmer voice, garnering a look from Meredith and a raised eyebrow from Burton. "Miss Wilde has expressed her unwillingness to accept your suit. Don't bother her again."

He turned then, taking Meredith with him and escorting her from the house and down the walk.

When they reached her buggy they stopped.

"I hope you know how grateful I am to you," she said, her eyes downcast. "I'm so embarrassed, and very sorry your day was ruined by all this. I was just so stunned when you arrived at the schoolhouse. Mr. Burton had left only minutes before. And when he walked in I thought it was you and I was so excited. I'd been waiting, you see."

"Meredith."

"I never stopped to think that by selling pies and cakes I would be offending him. I suppose that's a fault of mine. Perhaps I did use poor judgment. And then you were there and I was so upset that I wouldn't be able to have the desk and—"

"Meredith."

"After you left I regained my senses . . . well, not right away because . . . but I knew I couldn't let you face Elias alone. I knew so much more about him than you. He's a vile man."

"Are you through?" Michael lifted her chin, his eyebrow cocked. At her shy nod, he said, "Burton is nothing more than a little fish trying to make his way into a bigger pond. He's his own worst enemy, and he'll flap himself silly before he makes it."

She chuckled.

"As to helping, I'd do it again if you needed me." His thumb traced her jaw line. "But after seeing you in action I know you could have handled him yourself."

Her long lashes dropped. "It was nice not to have to do so alone. Thank you."

It was Michael who should have thanked Meredith, he told himself. He wanted to kiss her again, wanted to wrap her in his arms and tell her she'd never be alone again. "If you've got some time I'd like to talk," he said instead, and as the first snowflake fell he watched her nod her head.

Caroline raced down the stairs at Sarah's house and out the front door, shouting, "Come on, Sarah. Hurry!"

Sarah ran behind her, her breath coming in gasps when she caught up to her friend. "Where are you going? What's wrong?"

Caroline flew off the porch steps, her arms spread wide. She spun in a circle. "Snow," she cried. "It's snowing. I saw it from your bedroom window. Isn't it wonderful?"

"It's, brrr . . . c–cold." Sarah shivered and hugged herself. "Let's go back inside. Mama was making hot cocoa."

"No Sarah. Don't you see? Don't you remember? Now we can go skating."

"Skating? We can?"

"My pond is ready now. Papa said when it had snowed seven times then we could go skating on Buttercup Pond. Oh, Sarah, I've waited and waited and counted every time it's snowed and this is the seventh time. I marked the days on a paper just to be sure. Now I'll be able to remember my brother. Papa said if we did things like we used to do, we'd never forget. I need to go skating 'cause I can't remember him much anymore. And I think he'll come back, 'cause he went away the day after we were supposed to skate. He was mad at Mama 'cause she didn't take us skating like she was supposed to. He was always mad at Mama. Maybe she'll come back, too, but I don't think so, 'cause she wasn't like your mama. But Daniel will come. I know he will."

Caroline took a deep breath and stuck out her tongue to catch a snowflake. "Are you ready, Sarah? Are you ready to go skating and see my brother? Miss Red said your mama would probably let you."

Red was a bundle of nerves by the time they arrived at the schoolhouse. Michael opened the door for her to enter.

"Have a seat," she offered after they'd closed the door against the wind and swirling snow, locking themselves into the quiet room. She removed her coat and smoothed her hair and moved behind her desk as her nerves escalated.

"I'd rather stand," he answered. He lifted his hat from his head and raked his hand through his hair. Then he dropped the hat onto a wall peg and stood in place. When he turned to face her, his brow was knitted and Red's nerves tightened. His demeanor frightened her. She was certain she wasn't going to like what he had to say.

She clung to the memories she already had; their kiss, the way he'd stood up to Burton, the presentation of her desk. She knew not to expect anything else, and suspected he was going to tell her things had gone too far.

The sudden thought of him calling off her tutoring sessions with Caroline had her blurting out, "I realize I've been an imposition, Mr. Wisdom. I promise nothing of the kind will happen again. Please don't prevent Caroline and I from seeing . . . working together."

His gaze pierced her. Then he sighed and swept his hand through his hair again. "Claire wasn't a very good mother," he declared and Red dropped into her chair from shock.

"She was full of life, always laughing. But she'd been raised with money. Us marrying was the biggest mistake we ever made."

He walked to the chair facing Red's desk and sat down. She held her breath, silent, unable to say a word.

"I was just a carpenter. We lived modestly. She struggled to learn how to cook and clean, and her parents were always interfering. When Daniel came along, she gave birth at her parents' estate. When she brought him home a few weeks later she didn't know the first thing about caring for him. That's when I realized our marriage wasn't going to work out.

"She wanted me to take money from her father, badgered me to do so. But I was too proud. I gave in and let her hire a girl to help her, but that's when she started disappearing for hours, then days, at a time. She'd say she was going to a garden party or with her mother to the shore for a few days." He tapped his fingers against his pant leg. "After Caroline came along, she rarely held her. Was rarely home. Sometimes I wonder how she was conceived or . . ."

"You don't have to tell me this," Red finally whispered. She blinked back tears, her heart breaking for him.

"I was working more than I wanted, trying to make enough money to give Claire the things she wanted," he went on as if he didn't hear her. "Looking back, I realize nothing would have worked. Daniel . . ." He squeezed his eyes shut. "My son was on his own too much. Like Trip Dawson he was always coming home with scrapes and bruises. I didn't think much of them at the time. I was too busy. How I wish I had."

"Michael."

"The day before the fire—"

Fire? Oh, Lord.

"Claire had promised to take him and Caroline

ice–skating. As always, something interfered and she reneged on her promise. I learned later that Daniel was angrier than usual. He'd learned to live with disappointment most of the time.

"To soothe him, Claire agreed to take them to a circus that was in town the following day." He paused as if in reflection. "She was good at playing with them when she wanted to. I had a delivery to make, but I knew Daniel was upset, so I told them I'd meet them there. I was sure she'd have to keep her word then. We never did anything as a family, so the children were excited and happy.

"It made me realize that I'd been too busy and that I needed to spend more time with them. Especially since their mother rarely did. But I had this delivery to make first.

"If only Mrs. Bennett hadn't slowed me down to discuss some new pieces she wanted me to make. Talking to her made me late."

"Oh, Michael."

"When I arrived at the circus I couldn't find them. I thought they'd given up, already seen enough and gone home. It wasn't until I got home that I found out Claire had once again reneged on her promise.

"I just didn't think she would. Not when we had all planned to go. And Daniel . . ."

He paused. Red could see his incredible suffering reflected in his eyes. She began to tremble, the core of her chilled now.

"Our maid, Deidre, told me he ran out of the house when Claire came downstairs dressed for a luncheon. She was putting on her gloves and he grabbed one; they struggled, and he yelled at her, and then he ran away.

"He ran to our barn. On her death bed, Claire told me how she ran after him to try to calm him down. The glove he'd taken from her was already on fire by the time she arrived. He'd lit it on purpose.

"When he saw her it startled him, and he dropped it in the pile of hay where he stood."

A sob escaped Red. She fought down another.

"I could smell the smoke from a mile away. I had no idea it was coming from my own barn or that my son and his mother were inside. As I got closer, I could see the smoke."

"Please, Michael. I don't—"

"To her credit, she tried to save him. It was the one selfless thing she did in her entire life. She said Daniel ran from her. She lost sight of him in the smoke. Then the horses were going crazy and something hit her in the head. When I found her, she was unconscious. I didn't find Daniel until the fire was out. He was huddled in a corner of one of the stalls. If only he'd run toward his mother, they might have made it out." He stared straight ahead as a tear rolled down his face. Then he buried his head in his hands and was quiet for a long time. When he looked up he took a stabilizing breath. Red couldn't move and she could barely breathe.

"I loved her when I married her. She lit up a room when she walked into it.

"I thought we'd prove everyone wrong. But we were fools. I was a fool. She was from money and I wasn't. And I couldn't give her the life that she wanted. She needed maids and a housekeeper and a governess and a husband who moved in the same society as her parents did."

"But if you loved each other . . ." Red said.

"It wasn't enough. And it cost me my son."

"S–she would have matured, I'm sure," Red attempted to soothe. "S–she'd have realized her children were more important than parties."

"That's what I thought. Hoped for it for years."

"She didn't have the chance."

"She had more than enough chances." He rose from the chair, nearly toppling it. "And she realized it just before she died."

"She was sorry?"

"She was sorry." He looked at her, his face ashen. "Should that be enough?"

He was asking her?

"I haven't forgiven her, and I haven't forgiven myself."

And that was what was tearing him up inside, Red realized. "Oh, Michael," she cried. She rose from her own chair and went to him. Her hands shaking, she fought to keep from touching him. "You can't blame yourself for Daniel's death. You were just trying to provide for your family. And as long as you hold onto your anger for Claire you'll never get over the past."

"I don't want to get over it. I don't deserve to get over it. I should have been there. I should have known she'd disappoint them like she had so many times before."

"All right." Red decided to agree with him. She could see he wasn't going to listen to reason if she argued. "Maybe you should have postponed your delivery and taken the children yourself. And maybe I should have gone to Trip Dawson's house the morning he fell from the tree because I knew he wasn't working on his uncle's barn. I'm the one responsible for Trip's broken arm then.

"And my brother–in–law Sam, if you were to ask him, would tell you that he should have realized who murdered his sister long before the killer was discovered. He'll tell you it was his fault Julie died at the hands of her husband because she only married him to provide Sam a home."

Michael glared at her, moisture pooling in his eyes.

"I have other stories I could tell you. About Will and how he tried to steal April's land. About Travis and how he blamed himself for so many deaths during the war. May blamed herself when the railroad's payroll was stolen. And June—"

"I get it," Michael clenched his hands.

"Hindsight, Michael. We second–guess ourselves all the time. I had to ask myself if I'd really used poor judgment the way Elias Burton claimed. At first he made me think I had. But I did what I thought was right at the time. So did you. You thought Claire would follow through. You had no reason to believe she wouldn't take the children and meet you as planned."

His eyes shifted, as if he were considering her words.

"Forgive yourself, Michael. For Caroline's sake. For your sake."

He closed the distance between them with two steps and took her arms gently in his hands, pulling her closer. Staring at her with intensity that would have toppled her if he hadn't been holding her, he then brushed his knuckles along the outline of her jaw and softened his smoky gaze. An underlying current swirled between them. She felt herself moving forward, then backward, then forward again.

"You're a very smart woman, Meredith," he whispered. "Wise beyond your years. A prize for the man who claims your heart."

She could only stare at him, the urge to tell him he had already claimed her heart a mere breath away.

"Too often lately I wish I could be that man. I'm falling in love with you, Meredith. And I don't want to. Caroline already has. She'd be hurt again if you disappeared from her life like her mother did, and I—"

Michael stiffened.

"What?"

"Caroline," he said again. "It's snowing." His gaze turned thoughtful. "How many times has it snowed already this season?"

"I don't know. More this year than most. We usually don't get this much snow until . . . oh, dear God."

"Caroline," Michael breathed again just before he bolted for the door.

Chapter Nine

They took her buggy, not wanting to waste time unhitching horses from the rigs they were secured to. As dusk began to fall and snow surrounded them in swirling drifts, Michael steered the vehicle down the white powdery road. Red bundled herself into her wool coat and gloves and silently urged Honey to race as fast as she ever had. There were already two inches of snow on the ground and clouds hung low, blocking visibility, making the landscape ominous and foreboding.

Red couldn't imagine Caroline leaving the Caulders' in such weather. But if Michael's instincts were right, Caroline had been waiting for this day. She'd begged and begged to be taken ice-skating. Would she have told April that it was snowing for the seventh time this year or would she have left without a word? If so, had

Sarah gone with her? Sarah. Red would never be the same if anything happened to either child.

And yet hadn't she just been telling Michael that he couldn't blame himself for something there was no way to foresee?

"We'll get there in time," she whispered, more for her own assurance than for Michael's. She could see the utter terror etched on his face. Her words would have little impact on him. Not until he saw his daughter was safe. And if she wasn't . . .

Maybe the ice was thick enough. It usually didn't thicken enough until February or March, but this year the cold spell had already lasted nearly a month. It was possible the pond had iced over enough for her to skate and not fall through. Seven snowstorms before January were just as unusual, but the weather was always unpredictable along the Front Range.

Red kept trying to reason her fear away. It would do no good to panic. She needed to help Michael and be ready to help Caroline.

"We'll go straight to the pond," he told her decisively. "I'm sure she's still at the Caulders'."

"Of course she is."

"But I'm not going to waste time finding out."

"No."

"If we don't find her there, we'll head back."

"I'll stay at the pond just in case she's on her way there. You head to April and Will's."

"Good idea."

They fell silent again. Red wanted to reach out and touch him, but she didn't dare. Instead she began to pray.

Michael couldn't make the horse go fast enough to suit him. Nothing would have been fast enough to suit him, but the snow was making the rig swerve, which didn't help. His daughter was in danger and he was far away. Hadn't he sworn he would never put himself—or Caroline—in such a position ever again? And yet he had. He'd become too relaxed. How had he allowed that to happen?

He glanced at Meredith and knew. And he wasn't pleased about it. *I'm falling in love with you, Meredith. And I don't want to.* She'd distracted him, he'd dropped his guard, and now he regretted it.

It wasn't her fault. He'd just been captivated by everything about her. She was so different from Claire. Giving instead of self-serving, wise instead of foolish, dependable instead of irresponsible. She loved his daughter, a fact that had earned her more regard, and she cared about him. He wouldn't have been able to tell her the things he had if he hadn't known that. He'd never revealed to anyone the problems he'd had with Claire.

But in doing so, in wanting to take care of Meredith, he'd neglected his daughter.

Through the snow he saw the outline of his fence. He maneuvered the buggy through the open gate and held the mare to a steady pace. He brought the mare to a halt and jumped to the ground, then hurried around to assist Meredith.

"Go," she protested. "I'm right behind you."

He nodded and began to run. The pond was about a quarter of a mile from the house and fed by a natural spring. Native evergreens, pine trees, and wild grasses lined its eastern banks. It was shady in summer, offering a welcome respite from the heat. But today those trees and grasses would block his view and slow his progress.

"Caroline!" he began to shout when he saw the first of the trees through the snow. "Caroline! Answer me if you're out there!"

The landscape was as silent as he had ever heard it. There were no crickets chirping or toads croaking or coyotes howling. An ever–thickening bed of snow insulated the terrain, making him feel completely alone.

Had he been wrong to think his daughter would make her way to the pond without waiting for him to take her? Had he panicked? "Caroline?" he shouted again. He pushed his way through brittle tree branches still sprouting dead leaves, sending their snowy coats flying in all directions. His cold, booted feet plowed through the snow covering the ground. He finally broke through the last of the trees and stood on the bank. His hard breathing was the only sound breaking the quiet. Through the white veil his gaze darted from one end of the pond to the other but all he saw was blue–white ice topped with more powdery snow. There were no patches of cracked ice and no little girl in ice skates floundering in the frigid water.

"Thank you," Michael choked out as he bent over and tried to regain his breath. "Thank you."

"Michael?" he heard then. Meredith's frightened voice was not far away.

"This way," he called to her. "Caroline isn't here."

Her sob of relief reached him. He heard the rustle of branches as she made her way closer. When she emerged from the trees he wanted to grasp her, hold her, bury himself in her warmth and never release her.

He smothered his need instead. His infatuation with her had redirected his attention away from his daughter and because of it, he was standing by a frigid pond in the middle of a snowstorm fearing the worst.

"She's not here?" Meredith asked him, still struggling for breath.

"No."

"There's no sign of her?"

"None."

"Thank God."

"Yes."

She tucked strands of hair behind her ear and rubbed her frozen cheeks. Her gaze told him she was confused by his change of demeanor. "I'll stay here while you check the Caulders'. I'll search the area again just to be sure."

"Meredith, I—"

"We should have had more faith in her," she interrupted and blinked away sudden tears. "Caroline is smart enough not to—"

"Meredith."

She stopped talking and sniffed. He could tell she knew what he was thinking. "You think you dropped your vigilance, don't you? That you were preoccupied and didn't see the signs?"

"I'll take you home."

"No." Her tone was calm. She notched her chin. "No. I mean to stay here until you check the Caulders'. It won't take more than an hour. I'll wait for you and Caroline to return. Then I'll take myself home."

She was hurt. He'd hurt her. But he swore he'd never let anything happen to his daughter. Instead, he'd left her in the care of April Caulder several times over the past month and opened himself up to the possibility of another tragedy.

"You can't be with her every moment of every day, Michael," Meredith whispered as if she'd read his mind.

"She's my child, not yours. Don't tell me what I can and can't do," he lashed out.

Meredith stared at him. She wrapped her arms around her waist, warding off the cold. "You're right. And I'm sure she's waiting for you." She turned away from him then and plowed through the tall dead grasses to the edge of the pond. The water was iced over. It was probably an inch thick. But it needed to be much thicker to support a person's weight. Even a child's.

He shivered, thinking about what could have happened if Caroline had decided to go skating on her own. That image helped as he watched Meredith retreat. He couldn't risk losing Caroline. And if that meant losing Meredith, so be it. He'd been a fool to consider anything else.

She knew he was gone by the silence. The hush that settled over the land was so loud it was deafening. She heard blue jays and sparrows, cottontails and hares, does and bucks, and coyotes and foxes calling out their pity to her. Even the trees seemed to speak, their limbs extending out as if to envelop her in a hug.

They all knew what she knew: Michael had left her. He was so trapped by guilt and fear that he had decided he didn't have the capacity for anyone other than Caroline.

Red knew he was wrong. But she wasn't going to be able to convince him. She wouldn't even try. His demons were his own. He'd have to battle them alone.

Alone.

It could have been so different. They didn't have to be alone. They could have been a family and helped each other through the struggles of life.

I'm falling in love with you, he'd admitted. Her heart had nearly burst out of her chest when she'd heard those words. A future with him and Caroline and children of their own had flashed before her eyes. All the years would have been worth the wait.

But then he'd also said he *didn't want* to love her.

She'd ignored those words, hoping there would be more. *I don't want to, but I do, and I've realized I can't live without you.*

I don't want to, but since I do, I'm going to love you the rest of my life.

I don't want to, but you've come to mean the world to me.

A sob escaped her, and she buckled, the tall grass surrounding her as she sank to the snowy ground. Why had she ever thought *she* would be blessed in such a way?

"I am not going to sit here feeling sorry for myself," she said loud enough for the animals and the trees to hear. "If Michael doesn't want me, that's his problem."

A rustling behind her startled her. She spun to see two rabbits hopping through the brush. They stopped, glanced at her, and then kept going, as if commiserating with her.

She smiled sadly and then she got to her feet. There was no use thinking about things she couldn't change. It was still snowing, she was cold, and it would be a long while before Michael returned. She needed to move to regain some warmth and decided to walk around the outer banks of the pond.

Michael wrapped Caroline in his arms and squeezed. "Papa, I can't breath," she mumbled into his coat. Releasing her, he sat back on the toes of his boots as she giggled. "Did you forget you're so strong?"

"I guess so," he whispered back. He smoothed her hair.

"Is something wrong?" April Caulder asked from behind Caroline. They were all in the foyer of her home, her daughter in front of her, April's hands on Sarah's shoulders. He'd practically beaten the door down upon his arrival. After the door had opened, and he'd seen Caroline coming down the stairs to greet him, he'd nearly choked with relief and enfolded her in his arms.

April Caulder and Sarah had been right behind Caroline. Now April was gazing at him curiously. He was sure he looked a sight and that she could see the misery written on his face.

"Everything's fine now," he answered her. "I just . . . everything's fine."

"Papa, it's snowing again," Caroline intervened. "Do you know what that means? We can go ice–skating now. Right? I can't wait, Papa. I want to remember Daniel so bad, and you said we needed to keep doing things like we used to so we would always remember.

"Sarah and me asked Miss April if she can come to. Miss April said the a-a-adults had to check to make sure the ice was safe and then we could all go. Won't that be the bestest?

"Daniel will come, Papa. I know he will. And we'll both get to see him again."

"Caroline," Michael said, unsure of how to respond. He got to his feet, lifting his daughter into his arms. "I just came from the pond. I thought maybe you had gone there on your own because it was snowing and you thought you could."

"Oh no, Papa." Caroline's eyes widened. "I would never do that. I know I'm not supposed to. I could get hurt and that would make you sad." She cupped Michael's cheek in her hand and cocked her head, as if she were the parent and he the child. "Why would you think I would do that?"

He blew out a long breath. "I don't know. I was wrong to think so. Forgive me."

She wiggled for release and he set her down. "Sarah and me were making cookies with Miss April. We can bring them to the pond after you make sure the ice is ready. And cocoa and hot cider. Can I finish making them, Papa?"

"We need to go. Miss Red—" Meredith was back at the pond waiting for them. Cold. Worried. And after his return, he had to see her home and then return to the schoolhouse to unload the desk. Did he want Caroline out in the storm all that time? Just so she was with him? Just so he'd know she was safe? He glanced at April Caulder and saw the concern on her face. The house was warm, cozy, and smelled of nutmeg and cinnamon. It would be best for Caroline if she stayed right where she was.

"Would you care for a cup of coffee, Mr. Wisdom?" she asked.

"I would, ma'am. But I need to hurry. Meredith is waiting for me. We were worried . . . we thought Caroline might . . . she stayed behind just in case."

"Girls, will you go check on Caleb for me?" April

met his gaze as she spoke. "Don't wake him if he's still asleep. Then meet me back in the kitchen so we can finish our cookies. Caroline, why don't you ask your father if you can stay the night with us. That way we'll have plenty of time."

"Oh, Papa, can I, can I?" Caroline pleaded.

Michael maintained eye contact with April. "I think that's a wise idea," he said. He returned the hug his daughter gave him and watched her and Sarah race up the stairs and out of sight.

"Is my cousin all right, Mr. Wisdom?" April asked then.

"A bit worse for the wear, I'd say, Mrs. Caulder," he admitted.

"Then I think you'd better pass on that coffee after all and go to her. Your daughter will be fine until you return."

He tipped his head without another word and made his way back into the turbulent night.

Chapter Ten

Red sniffed and wiped her frozen nose for the umpteenth time with the handkerchief she'd retrieved from her skirt pocket nearly an hour ago, shivering and stomping through the ankle–high snow and damp earth as she kept watch for Caroline. Big fluffy snowflakes blocked all but her hand in front of her face, the pond nearly invisible before her. The wind was whipping around her face, and her face was wet from the moisture.

She'd circled the pond several times, trying to stay alert for traces of the girl, approaching voices, or the return of her and her father. The elements were making it difficult. She was so cold.

She'd begun to sing to herself to pass the time. Her mother had died giving her life, so Kit and a governess her father had hired had raised her. The governess, Mrs.

Neely, had stayed with them for fifteen years, but Kit had been the one to sing her a lullaby every night. Red sang *sleep peacefully sweet child, rest awhile, rest awhile* as she walked and heard Kit's melodic voice carrying from the past. She'd been a good sister, Kit had. She was still a good sister. Red would be lost without Kit and Sam and her cousins.

When the lullaby wore thin, she switched to her favorite hymn. She hummed "How Great Thou Art," while briskly rubbing her wool gloves together. She was watching her footsteps, wondering if her feet would ever thaw again when she heard, "Meredith!"

She swung around, her head snapping up at the sound of Michael calling. She didn't think there had ever been a time when she had been so grateful to hear another voice. "I'm over here," she answered, though where here was she wasn't certain. She retraced her footprints, moving toward the voice, knowing she'd reach him soon. She was surprised she hadn't heard his return, but then the snow had muffled every sound. "Can you hear me?" she called.

"Yes. You're getting closer." She could hear relief in his voice.

"Is Caroline okay? Was she with April?"

"She's fine. Where are you?"

"I'm coming. I've been circling the bank." She paused midstep when she saw his shadow through the snow. And then she began to shiver uncontrollably, her teeth rattling. "I–I–I'm glad you're finally back."

He pivoted and saw her. A veil of shimmering white separated them. "Meredith," he said again. "You must be freezing." He began to walk towards her. She let him. She was suddenly feeling too tired to move. Too numb to do anything but shiver and wonder if her body was reacting from the cold, anxiety, or both.

"Caroline's safe?" she asked once more when he halted in front of her.

"She wanted to know why I would think she was foolish enough to come out here alone."

"I k–k–knew s–s–she was s–s–mart."

"I wish her father was." He brushed the snow from her brow and nose while the snowflakes swirled between them and Meredith began to swirl with them. "Let's get you inside."

"T–t–that's a g–g–good idea," she said as her legs gave way.

"Meredith!" Michael caught her before she hit the ground. A limp rag doll in his arms, he scooped her up. Her breath was shallow against his neck. Her cheek was cold and clammy when he pressed his lips to it.

Blinking snow from his eyes, he began to walk toward his house, chastising himself all the way. Why had he left her alone? Why hadn't he realized it was too cold? What would he do if she took ill? Or worse?

How many times did he have to go through this?

"Wake up, Meredith," he whispered. "Please."

Her face was red from the cold. He could see bits of ice particles forming on the ends of her hair. He picked up his pace, laboring from the weight and the distance, but knowing every moment mattered.

He was winded by the time he reached his porch. He kicked the door with the heel of his boot, sending it flying open. The living room unfurnished, he had no choice but to mount the stairs and enter his bedroom, carefully placing her on his bed.

He threw off his own gloves, tugged at hers, tossing them aside. Then he began to breathe warm air onto her frozen fingers.

"Meredith," he urged. When that failed to rouse her, he proceeded to lift her foot, ever conscious of her modesty, remove one boot, the other, her stockings, and wrap her feet in a knitted blanket.

He left the room briefly, returning with a towel. He proceeded to dry her hair, free her from her damp coat and enfold her with more blankets.

"Wake up," he implored as he alternately rubbed her hands, feet, and arms. He tried to bank his concern and remain a gentleman while tending her, as well. But her lack of cooperation flustered and angered him.

"Fine," he finally said, defiantly. There was only one other way he could think of to quickly warm her. "But this better work," he added to himself. He shrugged out of his coat, tossing away propriety with it. If she needed warmth, he was going to give it to her. Lifting the blankets, he drew her into his arms, nestling next to her. The feel of her cold body was shocking. So was the desire coursing through him. He pushed it aside with difficulty.

"Take my warmth, Red," he whispered against her hair and kissed it. "Take my warmth. I'd offer you my love if I knew it was enough, but all I can give you is my warmth. Please take it."

When she groaned, Michael smiled. He cupped her face with one hand. "Can you hear me? Wake up."

She groaned again, a beautiful sound. "Hmmm?"

"You fainted. You're freezing. I'm trying to warm you."

Her lashes slowly lifted and he saw the irises of her incredible emerald eyes. He loved those eyes; he'd dreamed of them. From this very bed, they'd haunted him for weeks. Now she was in his arms, the way he'd imagined if not for the reason he'd imagined.

"Michael?"

"Shhh. You'll be warm soon. I'll head to the bunkhouse then and send one of the men to fetch Travis. Can you feel your fingers? Wiggle your toes for me."

Meredith's eyes widened, and she tensed.

"Yes, we're in my bed together. It was the only thing I could do. No one will ever know. Caroline is still at the Caulders'. No one is here except us."

He felt her relax, felt every curve of her body melt against his own. With a stifled moan he watched her flex her fingers, first one, then another. Then her foot stroked his.

"That's it," he breathed, even as his own body tensed. "Are you numb anywhere else? I–I've been massaging your arms. How about your nose?"

She wiggled it and he chuckled. Then her eyelids drooped and he was once again reminded of the seriousness of the situation.

"I'm going to light a fire now," he whispered. "If you're warm enough for me to leave you. Are you?"

Her eyes fluttered open briefly. "Stay," she whispered. "Please. Just a little longer." She snuggled against him, the emerald of her eyes burning a message of want into his own before she closed them. Michael lay beside her, his pulse rapid, his need strong.

His love was stronger. As much as he wished she was beside him for another reason, he would never take advantage of her. But he couldn't help but brush her still damp hair from her face with a caressing touch. He couldn't help but finger one of her freckles and marvel at its perfection. Her nose was still red but rapidly returning to its natural hue and her velvety lips were once again rosy instead of an awful shade of blue.

His heart beat to a normal tempo for the first time since leaving the schoolhouse, and he was assured now that, not one, but both of the females he loved were all right.

Of the two, he only had an obligation to one, his daughter. The other one had been tossed into his life when he'd least expected or been prepared for her.

I'm falling in love with you, but don't want to.

He still felt the same way. She deserved better.

He slipped away from her side while she slept on,

the chilled air invading his bones like the ache invading his heart.

On quiet feet he fed wood to the hearth, set it ablaze, and waited for the flames to chase the cold away.

He finally worked his boots back on while remembering the soft feel of her toes on his skin, and then he grabbed his coat and gloves and headed back downstairs. The door was still wide open, snow swirling into the foyer. He moved through it and slammed it behind him. He'd rouse Gavin from the bunkhouse and send him for Travis Worth. The doctor would find Meredith where he'd left her.

Assured that Red was out of danger, Michael could continue on to the schoolhouse.

Chapter Eleven

She sneezed and dabbed her nose with her handkerchief when she entered the schoolhouse on Monday morning.

Unsure of what she'd find, she paused in the doorway, her gaze immediately drawn to her new desk. She hadn't known until that moment what Michael had done with it.

Everything else remained the same: the children's desks, chairs, chalkboard. So why did everything feel different?

Bundled against the lingering winter freeze, she remained buried in her coat and gloves and crossed the room to the stove. Once the coal was heating, she walked to her desk.

She coughed, feeling it deep in her chest. Travis had

directed her to stay in bed for a few days. He'd awak-
ened her Saturday night when he'd been summoned to
assist her. She'd been surprised anew to find herself in
Michael's bed. And then she had remembered that
Michael had lain with her. She'd asked him to stay.

He'd obviously decided not to.

Travis had examined her, then bundled her for the
journey home. She'd obeyed his orders all day yesterday and watched the snow continue to fall outside her
bedroom window, and been pampered and cared for by
Kit and Maddie.

When asked for an explanation, she'd told them how
concerned Michael had been for Caroline's safety, how
she'd waited at the pond while he searched for her, and
how neither of them had realized just how cold the temperature had dropped. She'd kept the rest of the events
to herself. Everything from the confrontation with Elias
to the last moment she remembered with Michael—in
his arms.

Her emotions had run the gamut that day. The world
had been cut out from under her when Elias had dismissed her. It had rebounded when Michael became her
champion, crested when he'd told her he loved her, and
deflated again when he'd made it clear loving her was
not enough.

I don't want to.

The words still echoed in her mind. But as she ran
her hand over the smooth surface of her desk, she took
a stabilizing breath. She still had her classroom and stu-

dents like Trip. She still had her memories. More now. She would never forget waking in Michael's arms, wiggling her toes and fingers at his command, watching him smile. She'd never felt so warm.

She shivered now and sneezed again. And then the door burst open to startle her.

"Mornin', Miss Meredith," Trip said. "Heard you got stuck out in the storm the other night. Didn't know if you'd be here today."

"I wouldn't miss it, Trip," she said and meant it. Travis would probably reprimand her. Maddie had done her best to pressure her into staying home. But a day in bed had been all she could take. She'd found love and lost it only hours before. She couldn't remain in bed and think about it any longer.

"I'm glad you're all right," he added.

The classroom quickly filled with students, although several stayed home due to the storm. Red ignored her coughing and sneezing and began the day's lessons and thanked God for the diversion. It wasn't long before the day slid by; the children were leaving again and Trip was taking out his extra work.

Only then did Red wonder if Caroline would arrive. A half hour later, Caroline still hadn't shown.

"Maybe we should both call it a day, Trip," she said. "We've both been working hard, and I'm so proud of you, but we deserve a rest."

"Sure thing, Miss Meredith," Trip replied. "You should be home anyway."

"I should, should I? Is that the doctor in you talking?"

He grinned. Then he was grabbing his things and wishing her a good afternoon.

The quiet that enveloped the room after he left gripped her. There was no longer any activity, and she needed activity to keep her sorrow at bay.

Didn't Kit and Maddie and Travis understand that? She couldn't just rest. She hurt too much for that.

Giving in to her throbbing head, she placed her cheek on her desk. Maybe if she just rested for a minute. Then she'd rouse herself and find something to do.

She had just closed her eyes when the door creaked open. She pivoted to see Caroline standing in the doorway.

"Miss Red?" Her voice was tentative.

Red sat up. "Come in, Caroline. You're late."

"We didn't think you'd be here. We went to your house to take you some soup we made and Miss Maddie said you'd—"

"Disobeyed Doctor Worth's orders," Michael finished as he pushed the door wider and strode inside. His brow was furrowed as he strode across the room. "What do you think you're doing coming here today? Travis said you needed rest. He said you'd be home in bed. I can tell by looking at you that you're feverish. Your eyes are all glassy and your nose is red. We went to your place to bring you soup and you weren't even there."

Red sat up straighter, taken aback by Michael's

admonishment. "I needed to be here," she told him. It was true. "I suppose I must look a sight," she added and promptly sneezed, "but the children don't mind. And I listened to Travis; I stayed in bed yesterday."

"I could turn you over my knee, woman."

"You could what?" She squared her shoulders and narrowed her gaze. "What right do you have in managing my life? And just whom do you think you are, talking to me that way? You need to leave my classroom, Mr. Wisdom. And close the door behind you. You've let in a nasty draft."

Her words did nothing to dispel him. He took a step closer, the click of boot heels loud in her stuffy ear. "I'm the man responsible for your illness, Miss Wilde," he spat back. "Something I'm not thrilled about. And until you're well, I'm obligated to make sure you're being cared for."

Red chuckled derisively. "Responsible for my illness, are you?" She tried to rise, then reconsidered, her limbs too weak, but she could give him what for from where she sat. "You'd like to believe that. Just like you'd like to believe you're responsible for the world's woes, wouldn't you, Mr. Wisdom? You forced me to stay at the pond and wait for you? You tied me to a tree? Staked me to the ground? I'm responsible for my own illness, thank you very much. You don't get to claim this one. You'll have to find something else to load onto your back with the rest of the pile you've got there."

He looked at her, perplexed. "What did you just say?"

"It wouldn't do me any good to try and explain," she told him. She coughed, sneezed, and then said, "You're too late for today's session. In the future, make sure Caroline is on time."

"We didn't come for a tutoring lesson," he barked. He took his gloves and hat off, slapping them on the desktop. Then he leaned his hands on the surface. "Didn't you hear that we went to your house to take you soup?"

"We made it 'specially for you," Caroline put in. She stood several feet away, out of the line of fire. Her chin quivered.

Red smiled at the girl, trying to reassure her, but then she glared at her father.

"Miss Graham and some man I've never met before told us you were here," he went on. "What are you doing trying to teach when Travis told you to stay in bed?"

"Some man?" Red said, this time forcing herself to stand. "Smith Weatherby?"

"That was his name."

"Oh, my. I need to go." Red grabbed some books, then a few more and a pile of work she needed to review. "Oh, my," she said again.

"Where'd he come from?" Michael's tone was still irritated. "What does he want?"

Red bent down and kissed Caroline's forehead, ignoring Michael altogether. "I haven't been able to tell you how proud I am that you didn't go to the pond by yourself. And how glad I am that you're safe. But I have to go now."

"Papa said you were looking for me and you stayed at the pond in case I went there."

"I was and I did. And I'd do it all again if necessary." She shot Michael a look. "Take your papa home now, Caroline. And give him some of that soup you made."

She made her way to the door.

"Meredith," Michael called from behind her. But Red kept moving. Soup, indeed. A spanking, ha! And what was it to him if Smith Weatherby came calling? Maybe it would serve him right to wonder a bit.

She was already taking up Honey's reins when Michael and Caroline emerged from inside. Michael's fists rested on his hips and he was scowling. Caroline was suppressing a smile.

"Please lock up," Red shouted their way and continued to ignore his displeasure. She sneezed and hurried Honey down the snow–packed road.

"Meredith, dear, I'm so relieved you're home," Maddie said as Red walked through the door of her cabin. She rose from her chair and hurried across the room.

"Maddie, I heard—"

"You haven't met Mr. Weatherby, just arrived from

New York," Maddie interrupted. "Mr. Weatherby, Miss Meredith Wilde."

Only then did Red see Mr. Weatherby sitting in another chair. Kit stood as well, her hand on her back, her stomach protruding.

"Miss Wilde," Mr. Weatherby responded. "I've known your sister for years. I'm surprised we've never met."

"And I, sir," Red replied. "How do you do?"

"I'm a bit travel weary actually. But setting my eyes on Madeline again made the journey well worth it."

"Indeed." Red glanced at Kit. Her sister had stayed with her throughout the day yesterday until Sam had dragged her home. She was certain her brother–in–law wasn't pleased she'd returned.

"Sam will be here shortly," Kit said as if reading Red's mind. "We knew you'd be home within the hour, so I told him to return for me by four."

"You look done for," Maddie said to Red. Red felt Maddie's nervousness and wondered if things were going well with Mr. Weatherby's visit. He appeared to be friendly enough, and he had a kind face and warm features. She noted his receding blond hairline, the smoothness of his face, and that he stood level with Maddie. The cut of his clothing was impeccable. He emulated wealth and breeding, and he had a nice smile. "I've told Mr. Weatherby about your adventure and insistence on returning to your students."

"I admire your dedication," he nodded.

"Well, I am rather exhausted, I can assure you." She set the pile of things she carried on a sideboard and moved further into the house. "Hopefully nothing that a cup of hot tea won't cure. Let me welcome you to our home and Colorado. I hope you enjoy your stay."

"You're very kind."

"Mr. Wisdom brought you some soup," Maddie added. "That would help as well."

The reminder made Red frown. "So I heard." She wasn't going to elaborate. "Would anyone else like a fresh cup of tea? Kit, would you mind helping me?"

"Certainly."

Red waited for her sister before heading into the adjoining room. Once they were out of sight but still within hearing range, Red collapsed into a chair. "When did he arrive?" she whispered. Then louder, "I'll start a pot of water."

"I'll warm the soup Mr. Wisdom and Caroline brought you," Kit replied, before she whispered back, "He arrived just after you left this morning. Maddie greeted him at the door, but then told him he had to come to my house before she'd receive him. He agreed. In fact, he was eager to tell me his story. I listened, then thought Maddie should hear him for herself."

"Soup sounds delicious," Red said in a normal tone before she sneezed. She leaned closer to her sister. "And what *is* his story?"

"He confirmed that Lucia duped him. But her ploy was worse than anyone thought. When she told him she was carrying his child he couldn't even remember bedding her. But she swore he did one night when he'd had too much to drink. Since he couldn't prove her wrong with any conviction, he had no choice but to do the honorable thing. He later learned that not only was she not with child, but that he had never, you know, either."

"Oh, my."

"But by then they were already married. She'd wanted the security of his name, she told him."

A knock at the door halted their hushed conversation.

"It must be Sam," Kit said loudly. She waddled to the door. But upon opening it she stood back. "Mr. Wisdom. What a surprise."

Michael entered the house without an invitation. Red stared at him, seeing Caroline asleep on his shoulder. He scanned the living room, saw Maddie and Smith, then the kitchen, saw her, and headed for the sofa where he gently placed Caroline, covering her with a quilt before marching over to Red.

Kit closed the door and watched. Maddie and Smith both rose from their seats.

"We need to talk," Michael said to Red and grasped her arm.

Outraged, she tugged it away. "I'm doing no such thing."

"Don't wake Caroline," he warned. "She didn't get much sleep last night. She was too worried about *you*."

"At least *someone* was."

He scowled. "You think I enjoy being weighed down with guilt?"

She scowled right back. "I'm beginning to think so, yes."

"I don't. Get that straight. That's why I swore I'd never love another woman or have more children."

Maddie gasped. Kit as well. Red barely noticed. "You've made yourself more than clear, Mr. Wisdom. I'm not asking for your love or to have your children."

"You think I should just forgive myself. Move on. Start over."

"I think you should stop blaming yourself, realize that making mistakes are a part of life, and begin to live again."

"I have realized that," Michael raised his voice. It was Red's turn to shush him. "I've definitely realized that it hurts too much to care about people."

Red pursed her lips. "No, Michael, it doesn't hurt to care about them, it hurts to lose them. Isn't that how you feel? But, if you haven't noticed yet, none of us have any control over that. So we either accept it or we don't. You haven't accepted it."

"That's right. I haven't," he barked. "I don't want to accept that part." He fell silent then and Red took a step his way.

"Then you're going to go through life alone? Without trusting that you're strong enough to survive your losses?"

Tears shimmered in his eyes. "I couldn't stand it if I lost you or Caroline. I came close Saturday night."

"You've lost me anyway, Michael. And one of these days you might lose Caroline. You can't protect her forever. You have to let her go. But would you give up the years you had with Daniel? Do you wish you never had a son?"

"No." He closed his eyes.

"Are you going to give up the years we could have together too? Twenty, forty, sixty?"

"I don't want to give up another day."

Smith Weatherby cleared his throat. "I don't either, Madeline. That's why I'm here."

"Oh, Smith," Maddie exclaimed, and he kissed her.

Michael grumbled and reached for Red's arm again. This time she didn't try to stop him as he led her to the door that Kit opened for them to pass through. They skirted Sam, who was getting ready to knock. Kit embraced her husband and kissed him soundly.

Alone on the porch, Michael released Red and raked his hand through his hair. Red stood by and watched him take a deep breath.

"I started building a new table for the kitchen yesterday," he began. "And I thought about sending for some of the furniture I left stored in Philadelphia."

"That's nice."

"I could have used a sofa the other night. I didn't have anywhere else to put you besides my bed."

"I didn't mind."

He went quiet again, but his gaze seared her own. "You know this is tearing me up inside."

"Yes." When he didn't say anything else for several moments, she said, "Michael—" but he lifted his hand to silence her.

"I told you I didn't want to love you," he whispered. "But the fact is I do love you. I don't want to love you, because I'm afraid. How do I get around that, Meredith?"

"Don't be afraid," she encouraged. At the same time, emotion unlike anything she'd felt before made her tremble. She closed her eyes. She'd dreamed of hearing such words from him! "Please, Michael," she added, more prayer than statement. "Don't be." *Don't be so afraid that you throw away our love, our future together. Don't be afraid to live again. Please.*

He resumed his pacing, his brow creased, his gaze bleak and tortured. "I'll continue to blame myself."

"I know."

"I'll still question myself."

"Yes, you will."

"I placed you in danger the other night."

"You saved me."

"Will you forgive me when I fall short?"

"Always."

"Daniel . . . on his birthday . . . on the anniversary of his death . . ."

"We'll cry together."

He paused and stared at her. "He'd have wanted you for his mother."

She struggled for composure. "I would have wanted him for my son."

His nod was solemn. She felt a tear run down her cheek, knowing by all he said that the depth of this man was enormous. When he loved, he loved deeply. There was nothing shallow about him. He never gave half of himself.

"You'll marry me then?"

She blinked. It took her a moment to process his words. Then she smiled and cocked her head slightly. "No, Michael Wisdom. You'll marry me and be thankful you captured my heart."

He smiled broadly before standing toe–to–toe with her and wrapping his arms around her. "I've told myself many times that someday you'd make a very lucky man the prize of his life, Meredith Wilde. I never dared hope that man would be me."

He pulled her closer, smoothing his hands over her back. When his lips met hers, Red thought she would melt.

"Wisdom's prize," he teased after he'd broken the kiss. "I like the sound of that."

Epilogue

"Hurry, Papa! Hurry!" Caroline tugged on Michael's hand as they finished lacing their ice skates. "Look, Sarah and her mama and papa are already skating, and so is Miss Red and Miss May. Tommy and Mr. Luke, Mr. Sam, Mr. Travis and Matthew are going to beat us."

"I'm coming," Michael chuckled, trying to gain his equilibrium. It had been years since he'd worn ice skates. "We have all afternoon. Be patient."

"I don't want to be patient no more," she complained. "I bet Miss Kit and Miss June would already be on Buttercup's Pond too if they weren't having babies. You're too slow."

"Too slow, am I?"

"Miss Red, wait for us!" she called. "Hurry, Papa. I want to see Daniel."

"Now, Buttercup, we discussed this, remember?"

"Oh, I know, Papa. I understand now that Daniel is in heaven and that heaven is way far away and he can't come back. But when I skate I can still remember the times he skated with me, right? Like the time he skated by me real fast and knocked me down? And the time when that boy was being mean to me and he told him to leave me alone?"

"Yes, sweetheart. When you go places or do things you used to do with Daniel it will help you remember other times when he was with you, and those memories will bring him back again."

"Right. So let's go remember Daniel." She continued to tug on his hand.

"Yes. Let's," he smiled.

"What's taking you so long?" Red called from the edge of the pond. "The ice is great."

"I'm slow," Michael admitted.

"Well, we can't have that now. Can we, Caroline?" She took Michael's hand. "We need to get you up to speed."

Caroline glided onto the ice with a laugh. Michael pushed off and nearly lost his balance before righting himself.

"There, that isn't so hard, is it?"

"All right, you can stop teasing me now."

"Why, Michael, what a thing to say."

Caroline chuckled harder before she skated away.

"Hi everyone," Maddie called as she and Smith Weatherby arrived.

Red waved and tucked her arm around Michael's. He cupped her hand and they glided over the surface.

"This place sure looks different today than it did two weeks ago," he commented, remembering the snowstorm and all that had happened that day.

"It's much better today, wouldn't you agree?"

He took in the sight of everyone laughing and spinning and racing on the ice, of June and Kit and Maddie and Smith on shore, and of the woman close to his side. "I sure do," he said and kissed her cheek.

She purred and snuggled closer to him. "I hope this is the first of many winter picnics here. Your idea to invite the entire family was a good one."

"Actually, it was April who gave me the idea, so I can't take all the credit."

"April? How so?"

He smiled when he remembered April's subtle admonishment the night he'd left Red at the pond all alone. She had taken back her offer of a cup of coffee and told him to hightail it. He'd gone to apologize a few days later, and it was then that he learned all about the five Wilde girls: April, May, June, Kit, and Red.

"She told me about her mother, the first Sarah, and how she, May and June survived that first winter after her death."

"Yes, it must have been awful."

"April said she'd have never made it had her mother not instilled in her such strength and determination."

"My aunt called them God's wild flowers," Red recalled.

"Well, I figured I'd get an early start on spring and gather all His wildflowers together."

"You did, did you? And why is that?"

"Because you, your sister, and your cousins," he smiled, "all make a dreary winter day bloom like spring flowers."

2011
2010

2008
2007

2006